W9-ATO-192

Praise for

THE *POSTMODERN* PILGRIM'S PROGRESS

"*The Postmodern Pilgrim's Progress* is a fun, timely, and insightful read. If you're looking for an enjoyable read that also makes you laugh and think, this book is a must-read."

—**SEAN MCDOWELL**, Biola University professor, speaker, and author

"John Bunyan meets Paul Bunyan. A new alternative universe learns some tricks from the old imaginary worlds. And meatloaf finally meets cheese. Lots of laughs and lessons."

—**DALE AHLQUIST**, president of The Society of G. K. Chesterton

"Yes, this book is, as you'd expect, very funny and meaningful (the intro and first chapter alone had me laughing and crying—seriously), because it's written by two actual geniuses who I find myself in awe of regularly. But here's another thing: this book is IMPORTANT. I read the ending thinking, 'Please God, make sure so many people read this.'"

—**DALLAS JENKINS**, creator of *The Chosen*

"*The Postmodern Pilgrim's Progress* is a fun fantasy adventure with a lot of heart—and an important message, too. You will not be disappointed!"

—**KEVIN SORBO**, actor, producer, and director

"*The Postmodern Pilgrim's Progress* offers something incredibly important to people left adrift in a cultural moment that provides no fixed reference point for truth, meaning, love, or identity. Here, the fun we've all come to expect from two of the folks behind The Babylon Bee meets timeless wisdom and thoughtful insights on the human condition."

—**JOHN STONESTREET**, president of the Colson Center and host of the *BreakPoint* podcast

". . . people keep using terms like 'postmodern' and 'deconstruction,' and no one ever seems to be able to explain them. Kyle and Joel send you on an imaginative journey where you'll understand the other side and appreciate your faith . . ."

—**ERICK ERICKSON**, host of the *Erick Erickson Show*

"*The Postmodern Pilgrim's Progress* is a fun and witty laugh-out-loud fantasy . . . Just be advised that if you post that you like this book (which you will), the people who say they are fighting for 'inclusion, tolerance and diversity' will probably 'beat your brains out with a shovel' (see page 28)."

—**FRANK TUREK**, author, speaker, and president of CrossExamined

THE GREAT PLATEAU
BLACKMUCK WOODS
The King's Road
EVANGELION
DEPRESSION BOG
CITY OF DESTRUCTION

The River Infinite

THE GOLDEN CITY

PARADOX PEAK

TEMPTATION DESERT

VALLEY OF DOUBT

URBIA

THE DYING LANDS

N

The Postmodern Pilgrim's Progress

AN ALLEGORICAL TALE

Kyle Mann and Joel Berry

The Minds Behind The Babylon Bee

SALEM
BOOKS
an imprint of Regnery Publishing
Washington, D.C.

Copyright © 2022 by Kyle Mann and Joel Berry

All rights reserved. No part of this publication may be reproduced or transmitted in any form or by any means electronic or mechanical, including photocopy, recording, or any information storage and retrieval system now known or to be invented, without permission in writing from the publisher, except by a reviewer who wishes to quote brief passages in connection with a review written for inclusion in a magazine, newspaper, website, or broadcast.

Salem Books™ is a trademark of Salem Communications Holding Corporation.
Regnery is a registered trademark and its colophon is a trademark of Salem Communications Holding Corporation.

ISBN: 978-1-68451-275-1
eISBN: 978-1-68451-316-1

Library of Congress Control Number: 2022935263

Published in the United States by
Salem Books
An Imprint of Regnery Publishing
A Division of Salem Media Group
Washington, D.C.
www.SalemBooks.com

Manufactured in the United States of America

10 9 8 7 6 5 4 3 2 1

Books are available in quantity for promotional or premium use.
For information on discounts and terms, please visit our website:
www.SalemBooks.com

This book is dedicated to the quiet faithful, forgotten on Earth but remembered in Heaven.

And to the ones who struggle to keep moving forward, one obedient step at a time.

Soli Deo gloria

CONTENTS

AN INTRODUCTION BY THE NARRATOR

Go, go, go, said the bird: human kind
Cannot bear very much reality.

—T. S. Eliot, *Four Quartets*

Greetings, humans! Do you guys still say "greetings"? I've had a crash course on Earth languages over the past decade, but that's not quite long enough to fully grasp human speech. Oops—there I go splitting infinitives again! And of all your languages, English is especially tough. So plcasc forgive me if I don't get it all exaclly righl. Plus, your teenagers keep coming up with new words like "yeet," and honestly, it's just hard to keep up with it all, even for an essentially immortal being like me. Time, you know, has no meaning for me out here in eternity.

I won't bother telling you my full name. You wouldn't be able to pronounce it anyway. You can call me "The Narrator." My job is to chronicle stories—not just stories from your world, but across all worlds.

And I don't mean "worlds" in the way you might think of them, such as other countries, hemispheres, or planets—I mean other realities.

Oh, you thought yours was the only one? The seventeen-dimensional beings in Universe #XU-43B think that too, but they're also wrong. They're blissfully unaware of humans' existence, and I can assure you, that's a very, very good thing. You wouldn't want to meet them. It's not the sharp teeth—it's the laser pincers you have to watch out for.

I would describe what I look like, but I don't want to freak you out. I tend to have that effect on people. I've appeared to different humans through the ages, and they always react the same way when they see me. I've been wondering if I should tone it down a notch, but I do secretly enjoy the look of fear and wonder in their eyes.

I am a being created by the First Being. On Earth you might call Him a "pretty big deal." He spoke me into existence about 320,000 of your Earth years ago, so by celestial standards I'm pretty young. And now, He has tasked me with chronicling the dream of a young Earth-dwelling image-bearer named Ryan.

Humans are strange creatures, but I suppose you already know that. You have a crude organ in your skull that perceives and translates reality for you—but only a small sliver of it. You're like very simple radios tuned in to just one frequency among millions. A servant of The One Who Speaks once called your bodies "jars of clay." I think that's like dirt. I'll have to look that up. It was also a musical group in the 1990s and early 2000s, according to the Archives.

Oh, the Archives. That's where I work. It's a vast library, containing books without number. There are books on automobile repair, bungee jumping, gardening in space, and well over a trillion other topics. There are more useful, practical topics here too, like theology and philosophy. The theology section will never quite be complete, of course, since there is an infinite number of things to learn about the very object and originator of theology. Still, I try. My purpose is to gather information about everything under every sun in every galaxy in every universe.

But oh, the knowledge that is at hand here! If you image-bearers could only see what I see—well, things would be a lot different.

That's why I've been asked to write this story. It's a true story, and it all occurred within a dream, over the span of exactly 3.28 seconds as Ryan Fleming, thirty-three, lay on the purple carpet of a megachurch floor with a four-inch gash in his temple and a $5,000 video projector[1] smashed on the ground beside his head.

Don't be thrown off by the 3.28 seconds. Time in your little slice of the universe is not the same as time in the higher reality of the One who created me. What happened to Ryan was real and encompassed infinite lifetimes' worth of stories and eternal truths. The same things happen to you when you sleep, but the human brain is such a poor translator of reality. You can dive into infinite truths that transcend the physical universe during a nap on the couch, but when you wake up, all you'll remember is a salamander in a cowboy hat, or a giant cat destroying your house with his laser eyes. Or, more commonly, that you forgot to study for a test and that you're naked and all your teeth fell out.[2] Such limited creatures!

I have been given the unfortunate task of chronicling the adventure story you are about to read. I say "unfortunate" because it's really, really hard. You see, in those 3.28 seconds, Ryan will go on a journey in a wondrous place unbound by height, width, depth, or time. He will touch the eternal in a way that will change him spiritually and

---

[1] Projectors are like hymn books, except they are an average of 123,400 percent more expensive. They are used to help humans follow along with the music because their memories are very poor. The only thing worse than a human's memory is his attention span, which the projector remedies by adding flashing lights and pictures of clouds to the worship lyrics. It's odd that they even needed this, considering the song that morning consisted of a single line sung forty-eight times. Humans are such limited creatures.

[2] Of course, sometimes, these aren't real adventures in other realities. Sometimes, you just ate a bad burrito.

physiologically. There are an infinite number of things I could write about this adventure, yet I have to crunch it down into a few thousand words and a linear story so that your feeble human brains can comprehend it. See? Really hard. If you think editing a book or an essay for school is hard, try editing down infinity. It's a crying shame what you have to cut out sometimes.

On this journey, Ryan will learn something, which is more than most people who go on journeys can say. When he wakes up, he won't remember the dream, but he will be a changed man. He will be made new somehow, even if he can't explain exactly how. This will be the first in many thousands of dreams, interactions, moments, and strange coincidences that lead him to a moment every created being was created for: reconciliation with the Creator. The dream I am about to narrate for you is simply the one that kicked the whole thing off. We'll start with this one. It's more than enough. Baby steps. "Humankind cannot bear very much reality," indeed.

Someday (don't ask me the time and date because that's above my pay grade), you will see Reality face to face, but not yet. Hopefully this story serves to give you a dim reflection of Reality in the meantime—like one of those dim, dirty "mirrors" you humans love to stare at so very much.

And do leave me a review—I'm trying really hard to make this entertaining.

CHAPTER 1:

How a Megachurch Video Projector Catapulted Ryan into Another Reality

No one can tell what goes on in between the person you were and the person you become. No one can chart that blue and lonely section of hell. There are no maps of the change. You just come out the other side.
Or you don't.

—Stephen King, *The Stand*

There's nothing worse than visiting a new church and getting sucked into an interdimensional wormhole.[3]

Precisely twenty-eight minutes before Ryan Fleming found himself pulled through the floor of Ignite Christian Collective, he was pulling into the church's parking lot in his Honda Civic—an automobile only two decades old, though humans seem to regard any car more than a few years old as ancient. (It was new in the grand scope of eternity,

[3] Well, that's not quite true. This was my attempt to use the human form of speech known as "hyperbole." According to the Archives, there are at least 4,576,392 things worse than visiting a new church and getting sucked into an interdimensional wormhole, including going to hell, rubbing honey on yourself and jumping into the bear enclosure at the San Diego Zoo (which, by the way, will happen on March 4, 2062, dominating the news cycle for a full 12 hours), and watching an Amy Schumer comedy special.

but entropy in your universe works quickly.) Its engine whined and groaned, protesting as he screeched into the lot, clearly in some kind of hurry. The paint was flaking off the hood. The passenger window seemed to be held up by some kind of hanger wire and a heavy helping of duct tape.

Ryan's radio was blasting out a song by a band called Megadeth. I didn't get a good, hard listen at the tune, but it sounded like the guy was growling about bombs rusting in peace. It's true—they will "rust in peace" one day, by the way. Biblical prophets always get it right, but sometimes even the musicians nail it. The church's parking lot attendant waved a greeting as Ryan peeled out right by him, rushing toward the visitor parking and narrowly avoiding several families who were walking into the building.

Perhaps a little background is in order. Forgive my jumbled storytelling. Despite my occupation as a gatherer of stories, it's difficult to remember how each species retains information the best.[4] Since you humans prefer a more linear approach, let me back up and tell you about Ryan.

Ryan is the "hero" of this story, I guess. Honestly, he's one of the least impressive beings I've ever had to write about. In fact, I'll just read to you from his information card on file here at the Archives:

Name: Ryan Fleming
Age: 33 Earth years
Sex: Male
Hair color: Brown
Eye color: Brown
Height: 5'9"

[4] The most interesting cultural norm when it comes to narrative belongs to the hawk-people of Planet 27, Universe #4: they retain information best by eating the storyteller whole and digesting his brain matter for several millennia. I prefer the human method.

Weight: 165 lb.
Religion: Agnostic
Occupation: IT networking
Parents: Bob and Cindy
Siblings: Matthew, deceased
Favorite childhood cartoon: Animaniacs
Number of hairs on head: 112,994
Alcohol consumption: 25.8 liters per year
Pornography consumption: 73.2 hours per year
Pineapple on pizza?: N
Fan of *The Princess Bride*?: Y

You get the picture. I could go on; this card is pretty large, maybe the size of North America. And it's in seven-point font. Everything's on here. But I think I've covered the important stuff. If you need to know more, I can always pull his file again.

Despite being an agnostic, Ryan was attending church this brisk autumn morning because of a promise he'd made to his brother, Matthew. The dead one. (Sorry—was that harsh? Empathy isn't really a strength of my particular species.) Matthew Fleming, Ryan's much younger brother, had died on a Sunday exactly two weeks prior. Matthew's countdown to death had begun at age fourteen when an astrocyte cell in his cerebrum produced a DNA copying error that began to multiply unchecked. It produced a lump of useless tissue whose only purpose was to grow and spread through its host. You call it brain cancer. There are several billion volumes in the Archives that discuss the "how" of cancer. There is only one volume, however, that discusses the "why," and I'm not allowed to read it. So don't bother asking me why. (Sorry, I know—empathy. Working on it.)

In the interest of empathy, let me try to relay the story from Ryan's point of view with few interjections.

Within a few months, the cancer had produced tumors in Matthew's brain and spine. It ravaged his body and mind and ripped him away from your world after two years of stealing his memories, altering his personality, and muting his speech. It had been a horrific two years. By the end, there wasn't much of Ryan's little brother left.

On the day of his death, in one of Matthew's rare coherent moments, he had begged his big brother to start going to church again. Ryan wasn't sure if it was some random firing of Matthew's ravaged synapses or a genuine request, but either way, his words had been clear enough.

Go to church again, Ry. Just do it. Promise me you will, at least once. I wanna see you again someday.

Ryan felt disgusted by his little brother's emotional manipulation even in death, with the all-too-common carrot of some glorious afterlife in which you'll see your loved ones again and walk on streets of gold. Ryan had never understood the appeal of streets of gold. Asphalt worked just fine. But still, little Matty's approach worked. Ryan loved his brother. He had looked down at his frail body at the end and said, "Yes, I will," as bitter tears streamed down his face.

What else could he do? His brother, born when Ryan was a sophomore in high school, was his joy. He hadn't had a sibling before. Matt looked up to him, the cool brother, the young adult who had a car and a girlfriend and could take him to the movies and the batting cages and the Boomers Fun Park mini golf course and youth group. Ryan, in turn, found a sense of purpose in making sure Matt was safe from the cold reality of the world.

Matt had found Jesus (or, if you prefer, Jesus found him)[5] when he was fourteen, at some summer camp where parents sometimes drop kids off when they don't know what else to do with them. Ryan found

---

[5] Don't start. I'm not going to have that argument with someone who only has a human-level intellect. It would be like arguing with a drunken toddler.

it a bit annoying but chalked it up to a stage that would soon pass. The stage never passed—it never had a chance to. Three weeks after Matt came home from camp, he started complaining of headaches.

The next two years were a blur—a slow-motion horror show of scars, staples, tubes, loose hair, and slurred, broken speech. Ryan watched as the "God" his little brother claimed to love so much tortured him slowly and then snuffed out his life on a hospital bed in front of him, his mom, and his dad.

Let me pull up Matthew's death scene from the Archives . . . ah, here we are. Matthew Fleming's Entrance into Eternity, Perspective: Ryan's, May 6, 2016:

Ryan and his parents are sitting at Matthew's bedside. Matthew's shrunken, pale body lies before them, tubes and wires and needles sticking out of him like some kind of mad scientist's experiment. Matt's youth group leader from church has just walked in—dressed, as always, as if he just returned from a shopping spree at Forever 21.

Matthew: —gonna be alright guys. I promise.

Youth Leader: That's right Matt! We can do all things through Christ who strengthens us!

Ryan (under his breath): Will this guy please just shut up or go away?

Matthew: Well, I don't know if I'll be alright, but I feel like that's what I'm supposed to say. Go to church again, Ry. Just do it. Promise me you will, at least once. I wanna see you again someday.

Ryan: Yes, I will.

Matthew: Ryan . . .

Ryan: What, Matty?

Matthew: Walk forward. Sometimes all you can do is move forward.

Ryan, thinking to himself: What on earth is that supposed to mean?

Matthew: Mov . . . Mrrr . . .

Matthew makes a weird face and looks off to the side at an empty corner of the room. He's gone again. Ryan can always tell when his brother is gone. Sometimes he just goes somewhere else. The tumor just seems to erase him. The light leaves his eyes. Sometimes he comes back a minute later. Sometimes days later. And very soon, he won't come back at all.

"Matt . . ."

Their mother collapses on the bed, sobbing.

Youth Leader: It's OK, Mrs. Fleming! God has a plan! He'll never give us more than we can handle!

Mrs. Fleming: THIS IS MORE THAN I CAN HANDLE! THIS IS MORE THAN MY SON CAN HANDLE!

Bells go off. Voices call out over the loudspeaker. Doctors rush in. Ryan and his family are rushed out. One of the nurses jumps on the bed and starts pushing down forcefully and rhythmically on Matt's frail little chest. More shouting. A sternum cracking. Blood running out of Matthew's nose.

Minutes pass.

Everyone slows down, then stops.

One doctor walks out of the room and removes his mask. He tells everyone what they already know.

Time of death: 1:37 p.m. PDT

Ryan's little brother is gone, but all he can think about are the words of that youth leader who has since slipped out: "God will never give you more than you can handle."

Why, God? Why?

Maybe as a human, you can relate to Ryan's feelings right now. I can't. If I had the capacity to doubt, that might cause me to doubt as well. But, you know, I've seen the Creator. Actually, let me amend that: I've seen a blinding light and fallen on my face as the ground shook all around me and smoke surrounded me in an overwhelming display of holiness, of ultimate otherness. Anyway, take my word for it: He's real. Frighteningly so. And Matt? Don't worry about him. He's completely fine. Never better, in fact.

But this is Ryan's story, not Matthew's. The weeks since his little brother's death have been filled with drinking, showing up late to his soul-crushing IT job, late-night porn binges, and ignoring texts from friends. He has a couple bottles of his brother's leftover pain medication on his bedside. Maybe he'll take it tonight, all at once, and check out forever. Why not?

But he has one thing to do first, and that is to attend church. One last promise to fulfill for his brother. He googled "churches near me." He picked the one at the top of the list: Ignite Christian Collective.

He slumped into his "old" car and sped off to church, his radio blasting that prophetic heavy metal.

Ryan parked his car in the first-time visitor's parking section of Ignite and took a deep breath. A bit of sunlight peeked through his partially open window and hit his face. It felt good. *I'm gonna try to enjoy this*, he thought. This particular American megachurch didn't have much genuine truth to offer Ryan or anyone else. Still, he was trying, and trying often counts for much more than you'd think. He parked his car, took a deep breath, and got out.

"Here we go," he muttered under his breath.

He took a few steps toward the front door of the church—sleek, modern, angular, with brushed steel, premium rock, and hundreds of reflective glass panels—and stopped. He walked back toward the car, opened the passenger side, and rummaged around in his glove compartment. He found what he was looking for: an old but barely-opened Bible his mom had given him on his eighteenth birthday. He wasn't sure why he'd kept it—just a reminder of a simpler time, he supposed.

Ryan took a deep breath and turned back toward the church. The glass-steel-rock monstrosity had a towering steel cross suspended above the entrance, which was one more cross than most megachurches had those days. Without the cross, you might have mistaken the place for a shopping mall. A banner flapping in the crisp early-autumn breeze declared that the church's current sermon series was called "Choose Happiness!"

Ryan tried to look casual as he walked toward the entrance, as though he belonged. He kept his head down, not wanting to make eye contact with the all-too-cheery church greeters.

"Welcome to IGNITE! We're so glad you're here!" one chirped in his direction.

Aw, crap. They've spotted me. Maybe if I stay really still—is their vision based on movement?[6]

"I'm Tad. What's your name, son?"

"Ryangoodtomeetyou," he muttered, taking a program and hurrying off as fast as he could. The last thing he wanted right then was small talk.

The church foyer only reinforced the shopping mall comparison. There were booths manned by smiling faces, a few dozen people milling about, a cafe with artisanal coffees and a full lunch menu, and a sprawling bookstore. A tall banner declared that the pastor had a new book, *Claim Your Victory, Reclaim Your Life*, coming soon. The pastor, hair slicked back as though with motor oil, gazed at him from the banner like a creepy dictator ruling over some future dystopia. Straight ahead were the looming steel doors to the sanctuary. Haze billowed out from underneath them as the thrumming bass vibrated out from the ongoing service, the worship leader singing something about how reckless God's love is along with lots of fire and water metaphors.

---

[6] This is apparently a reference to a film called *Jurassic Park*, in which humans create a dinosaur theme park and get devoured. I looked it up in the Archives. Funnily enough, this actually happened in Universe #523B, though it was dinosaurs creating a human theme park. Sometimes novelists and filmmakers get ideas in their dreams as they have visions of other worlds, but they don't always get the details right when they wake up.

To Ryan, religion was just a way for humans to cope with the truth that there was no truth out there, no meaning for anything that happened. And everything he saw in this fake church full of fake people just confirmed his opinion.

"Welcome to IGNITE! We're so glad you're here!" another too-happy church greeter practically shouted in his face. Ryan wiped the man's spittle from his brow.

"I've got some great news! As a visitor, you get a complimentary donut!" He was handed a piping hot Krispy Kreme donut. "Would you also like a free artisanal coffee at our cafe?"

"No thanks."

"How about a free copy of our pastor's new book: *Claim Your Victory, Reclaim Your Life*!"

"No."

"Oh." The greeter seemed crestfallen.

Ryan had to get out of there. He muttered something like an apology and slipped into the sanctuary, welcoming the darkness of the massive room.

It was hard to tell if he'd entered a Deadmau5 concert or a church service. Lasers blasted every which way like some European EDM festival. Haze surrounded him, enveloping his body in a cold, foggy soup. The people he could see in the glow of the stage lights raised their hands and swayed back and forth like palm trees in a tropical storm. The worship band featured eight or nine members, all decked out in the latest style.[7]

"Oh, the devastating love of Goooood!!!" the worship leader sang in a ridiculously high key. He closed his eyes tight, as though he were experiencing the very presence of the Lord (he wasn't). "Take us away in Your love hurricane! Burn us up in Your love inferno!"

---

[7] I've studied human fashion before, and *man*. Let me tell you. Things really peaked about eighty years before this, when men all wore hats. Everything went downhill when men stopped wearing hats.

"Not literally, I hope," Ryan muttered. He looked for a seat in the back, but he was far too late to the service to secure such a prime spot. He moved forward, squinting in the darkness, looking for a seat, any seat. "Oh no."

There was only one seat he could find: right in the front. A smiling usher spotted him and waved him toward the front row with a little airplane-signaling baton. Resigned to his fate, Ryan slipped into the prominent spot as quickly and quietly as he could.

What Ryan didn't know was that directly above him, about thirty feet up, was a Panasonic projector that displayed lyrics to the songs on the screen in front of him. Encased in black aluminum, it weighed about ten pounds and hung from the ceiling by a metal rod bolted to the steel rafters. I have never understood the human need for these things. Your worship songs are four words repeated thirty-two times and you still need a visual cue to remind you where you are in the song. Such limited creatures.

Anyway, this particular projector had been installed two years prior by a tired, seventy-two-year-old electrician named Hank Billings at the end of a long day. He had forgotten to include lock-washers that would keep the bolts from loosening. Two years of pounding bass vibrations had loosened the bolts to the point that it was precariously dangling above the spot where Ryan was standing.

Ryan nibbled at his donut as the worship team finished up their closing power ballad. Ryan dutifully closed his eyes as the worship leader prayed to introduce the sermon. When he opened his eyes again, the worship team had vanished as if by magic. In their place stood a man who could only be the pastor: plunging scoop-neck tee, $400 haircut, designer jeans, and shoes that cost more than Ryan's Civic. He stood there enveloped in a mystic fog like Yoda, or maybe one of the swamp creatures from the Dagobah System. A synth played a single, sustained bass note drawn out as if they were all in some sort of Shaolin temple.

Gimme a break. Ryan rolled his eyes.

The teeth-chattering bass vibrated Ryan's rib cage, as well as the bolts holding the projector in place.

The bolts got a little looser.

"Hey y'all—you can grab a seat. Who's ready to get into the WORD!" the preacher said. Scattered hoots and hollers. Someone near the back of the room boomed an "Amen!"

"Wait—what was that? I can't hear you! Come on, is this a Presbyterian church? I didn't come to preach to no frozen chosen today!"

More enthusiastic cheers. A few louder "amen"s.

"That's right, that's right. Alright, fam, today, I want to talk to you about suffering, about grief"—Ryan's heart caught in his throat—"and why real Christians say 'no' to these kinds of negative emotions!"

"Mmmhmmm."

"That's right."

"Preach it, pastor."

"Anyone in here who's sufferin'—guess what? All you gotta do is just! Say! No!" The crowd chanted this mantra along with him, so it must have been a regular slogan for this "pastor." "That's right, fam! You gotta reach inside yourself and find the positive. Jesus didn't come so you could walk around feeling bad about yourself! You gotta look suffering in the face and say, 'Not today!' And when you do that, as we're gonna see today in this message, when you do that, life falls into place. You'll be successful!"

Is this clown serious? Ryan thought. *How rich has he gotten spouting this nonsense to people?*

"Yeah!" The crowd was really getting into it now.

"You'll be financially stable!"

"Yeah!"

"You'll be healthy!"

"YEAH!"

And then, the pastor said those words. The words that had been echoing in Ryan's head ever since his brother had died so pitifully. The words that had been uttered by the Forever 21 youth pastor at Matthew's bedside.

"God will NEVER give you more than you can handle!"

Ryan felt his face flush with anger. He wanted to leap up on the stage and grab that guy by the neck.

The bass notes thrummed. With a squeak, the projector loosened a little more.

The pastor repeated: "Did you hear me? God will NEVER give you more than you can handle!"

"LIAR!"

The word seemed to leap out from the pit of Ryan's gut. He didn't really mean to, but he spoke out loud. Very loud. So loud, in fact, that the entire front section heard it. The pastor heard it.

The place went quiet. If this had been a TV show, this is where you'd hear the "record scratch" sound effect. The tension in the room thickened. The squeaky projector mount loosened.

The preacher man in his $400 shoes and equally expensive haircut stared daggers at Ryan, right in the front and center.

"What was that, young man?"

"I said you're a liar!" Ryan said hoarsely, his emotion getting the better of him. "What can you possibly know about suffering?"

The audience gasped. A sound guy cut the live feed. From the back of the auditorium, security guards started making their way up to the front.

It was too late to turn back now. Ryan didn't care who was watching. Now, the rage of the last two weeks poured out of him. "God isn't real! YOU aren't real! None of this is real! So screw you and your . . . your . . . stupid haircut! You look like a complete idiot!"

The pastor was flummoxed. Clearly, no one had contradicted him before, at least not since he'd taken the helm of this church. It was also quite clear no one had insulted his haircut before, either. And especially not in the middle of a sermon.

He paused and looked at Ryan thoughtfully. He slowly raised his microphone to the side of his mouth, much in the style of the musicians who perform "rap," a genre of human "music."

The pastor cracked a sly smile as if he were about to drop a killer verse. Right on cue, the thrum of the bass resumed. A bolt fell from the projector mount above, and it shuddered, causing the song lyrics on the screen to vibrate ever so slightly. No one noticed.

"Give this young man a microphone!" the pastor said. "I believe today is a divine appointment for him."

Scattered applause from the congregation, who still didn't know what to think.

"Come on. We don't bite. I believe God has a divine plan for you, and I want to find out what it is."

A beefy security guard with an Agent Smith-style earpiece[8] walked up and tensely handed Ryan a microphone, apparently ready to bear-hug him and drag him out of the building.

"What do you have to say for yourself son? And please—no bad language."

Ryan took a deep breath. "I mean . . . I just . . . Look, life sucks, OK? Life is suffering. It's not a fairy tale. The rest of the world, we deal with that. We try to process grief and tragedy and . . . and family members dying in hospital beds even though they're the nicest people in the world. You'd think you all could accept that, but no. Not you. You build this stupid Willy Wonka place so you can pretend the real world doesn't exist, but it does! God doesn't exist. We are on our own. If He does exist, He's either powerless, or—or else He's just a huge jerk. My little brother died a horrible death for no reason. There's no

---

[8] A reference to the human movie *The Matrix*, which is actually based on a true story from universe #TB-22I.

plan here. We're animals. We live and we die, and that's it, and it sucks. You people are delusional."

Ryan wasn't sure if he was making sense. The words just kind of poured out of him. He was trying to hold back tears but couldn't. The audience just stared at him, a thousand eyes in the dark. The preacher still stood there—clearly, he had gotten more than he'd bargained for. Finally, he eyed another security guard who began to close in on him from his left.

Well, I guess my time's up, Ryan thought.

The projector fell.

CHAPTER 2:

A Hole in Reality

The most merciful thing in the world, I think, is the inability of the human mind to correlate all its contents. We live on a placid island of ignorance in the midst of black seas of infinity, and it was not meant that we should voyage far.

—H. P. Lovecraft, *The Call of Cthulu*

Space is big. You just won't believe how vastly, hugely, mind-bogglingly big it is. I mean, you may think it's a long way down the road to the chemist's, but that's just peanuts to space.

—Douglas Adams, *The Hitchhiker's Guide to the Galaxy*

The human brain is a crude organ, wrapped in an even cruder shell of bone, scalp, and hair. Surprisingly, it can withstand a lot of abuse, but a hit from a ten-pound hunk of metal falling from two stories above is kind of a toss-up. This will kill some people, and the ones who survive . . . well, let's just say it ain't pretty.

Thankfully for Ryan, the state-of-the-art Panasonic LCD projector didn't hit him squarely on the top of his head. It only *kinda* hit the top of his head, grazing him along the side of his face and cutting a four-inch gash in his temple. It also knocked him out cold for 3.28 seconds. And Ryan dreamed. A whole 3.28 seconds of dreaming is a ton of material to cover in one book, but I'll do my best to condense it down for you.

The projector struck Ryan's head and crashed to the ground in a shower of sparks and twisted metal, crumpling Ryan to the ground along with it.

And then he kept falling.

He braced himself for a painful collision with the floor of the church, but it never came. He fell through the carpeted floor of the church, through a layer of concrete, and into the earth. *OK, this is weird,* he thought, which is the appropriate reaction to getting conked in the head with a video projector and falling through the floor of a megachurch. Everything was completely dark, and yet he kept falling.

He tried to cry out, but he couldn't hear his own voice. All was silent. He was still falling, his arms flailing in the dark. And he could feel his body accelerating.

Stars and galaxies filled his vision, numerous as particles in a dust cloud stirred up by the wind. An entire universe of galaxy clusters and nebulae opened up before his eyes, then suddenly flew past as if they were as small and insignificant as the dust itself. More stars. More galaxies. Ryan felt as though he were sitting in the world's most blindingly detailed planetarium show, played at triple speed. His vision began to warp just like in the movies when a starship jumps to light-speed while smuggling spice from Kessel or boldly going where no man has gone before.

I must be jumping to lightspeed, Ryan thought, and he was correct on this count.

He could no longer feel his own body moving. His vision was no longer filled with stars and galaxies. It was filled with faces, feelings, memories. It moved faster and faster, each vision whipping past in a fraction of a millisecond. His life was, almost literally, flashing before his eyes as he shot through the cold blackness of space like a cork from a bottle.

And then, suddenly, he crashed into something solid.

Well, it wasn't actually solid, but it sure felt like it. This is the point when Ryan left Universe #531-C, where your home planet resides.

Other travelers have said it feels like water, or rather, like hitting the water after being dropped from a helicopter at three thousand feet. Ryan had just performed an awkward belly flop into another universe. Just like a belly flop into a pool, this was painful. Ryan suddenly felt his body again, or what was left of it. He felt as if every bone, every muscle and tendon, had been crushed by a meat tenderizer, turned inside out, shredded, and crudely reassembled. Whatever was left of him was still flying.

He could see galaxies again, but these looked different. Instead of the spiral, organic-looking galaxies he was used to, these formations had very specific, recognizable shapes. Some were pyramids. Some looked like animals. Some looked like the faces of creatures he didn't recognize. All of them seemed to be moving, as if they were alive.

Then, finally, something familiar. At least kind of familiar. A blue planet came into view. It was somewhat Earth-like, with green patches of land and blue stretches of water.

And he was heading right for it.

Ryan hit the atmosphere at breakneck speed, and while painful, he felt a sense of relief to see his body was still intact. He could feel his arms and legs again. In his peripheral vision, he could see his fingers and toes. *Phew, they're still attached.* He rocketed through the atmosphere, through a layer of clouds, and then he hit the water.

The ocean engulfed him, but he did not die, or this would be a very short story. He plunged into an icy-cold blackness and suddenly realized he needed to breathe. All he could think was that he needed air, and he needed it now.

Light! Ryan was sure he saw light, somewhere above or below or beside him, and he made desperate strokes in what he thought was its direction, hoping against hope it was the sun in this strange alien sky. His vision began to go black, first in spots, then in waves, and finally in pulsing, all-encompassing sheets of unconsciousness. He knew he had one last desperate chance, and he kicked and pulled against the crushing weight of the ocean with his final shred of strength.

It worked! He pierced the surface of the raging waters and gasped, taking the wildest, deepest, most refreshing breath of his life. He whirled and thrashed, knowing that he'd need to find solid ground soon or be lost in the icy oceans forever. By some stroke of luck or fate, he glimpsed land above the swelling of the sea, an outcropping of sand and rock some hundred yards off. He wasn't a great swimmer, but you'd be surprised what the fear of death can motivate you to do in a pinch. He swam for the shore with all the grace of a water buffalo, but he seemed to be making progress until, at long last, a mighty wave cast him upon the sandy shore.

He crawled from the waves, scrambling by some merciful shot of adrenaline up out of the reach of the ocean's fury just before a much larger wave crashed upon the sand and rock. While the angry waves of the sea missed him by mere inches, the waves of unconsciousness finally overtook him, and he slept.

Hours or days or weeks later—he didn't know which—Ryan woke up in a warm, comfortable bed. His head was throbbing. Actually, his whole body was throbbing.

"It's safe to say I'm never visiting Ignite Christian Collective again," he said to no one in particular.

He felt his head. A tender bump had appeared on his right temple, like the ones Wile E. Coyote got in the cartoons.

"What a crazy dream," he muttered.

He slowly rose, rubbed his eyes, and looked around. His heart stopped and his stomach lurched. He had no idea where he was. He was no longer in the church, and he was no longer on the beach. He was in a house, but it was unlike anything he had ever seen. Alien.

The walls were made of gray stone of oddball sizes, like a castle wall built by a maniac. The roof above him was low and humble, solid wood, crudely built. He had been lying on a bed of straw. Warm yellow light filtered through a window with wooden shutters, cracked open two or three inches. Dust danced in the beams.

His mind started to come back. *This is my room*, he thought. *This is my house!*

He remembered his name again. *Christian. Christian.* Of course. Christian from the City of Destruction.

Then, another thought, another memory, collided with his mind: *No! I'm Ryan—Ryan from the San Fernando Valley.*

The San Fernando Valley? That sounds made up, the other voice said. *You live in the City of Destruction. You've always lived here. Your name is Christian!*

As the name "Christian" entered his mind, a flood of scattered memories came with it. Visions of visions, dreams within dreams. He was running and hiding—from what, he couldn't remember. He saw his own feet frantically trudging through snow. He saw the face of a king. And with the memory of that face came a feeling of shame.

"No!" he finally shouted. He grabbed his throbbing head. "I am Ryan from L.A., and this is nothing but a dream!" He looked down at his body. He was wearing a loose white robe—possibly underclothes—made of a rough, itchy material. Beside his—Christian's?—bed lay a crumpled pile of clothes more suitable for going outside: a leather tunic, sturdy brown leather pants, a faded green cloak, and a well-worn pair of boots.

Ryan gathered up the clothes and put them on. They fit well, though it felt like wearing the clothes of a sibling he'd never met. He headed for the wooden door at the other side of the room and stepped out into the sunlight.

The first thing he noticed was how calm and peaceful the town was: a perfectly quaint village full of happy townspeople. It was arranged like a wheel, with the streetways jutting out like spokes from the center, where a stone well was set and traders sold their wares under colorful banners set atop their market stalls. A black-haired, fair-skinned woman drew water from the well. A boy no older than twelve with sandy hair and freckles whistled a tune that reminded him of John Lennon's "Imagine"[9] as he pulled a cart full of strange red fruits shaped like U's right past Ryan.

The second thing he noticed was the flaming meteorite hurtling toward the house he'd left moments before.

---

[9] "Imagine" is a song about a horrifying fantasy world where there's no Heaven, no Hell, no religion, no countries, and no enjoyable melodies. Thankfully, according to my records, no such place exists in the many universes the Crafter of Realities has yet made.

CHAPTER 3:

THE CITY OF DESTRUCTION

Their end is destruction; their god is their belly; their glory is in their shame.

—The Apostle Paul, Philippians 3:19

That's it, man! Game over, man! Game over!

—Pvt. Hudson, *Aliens*

Ryan spotted the crimson streak of light not a moment too soon and leaped out of the way as the piece of rock and twisted metal crushed his home—Christian's home?— into oblivion. Red-hot rock and charred, smoky wooden beams flew in his direction as he scrambled to his feet and ran, screaming, toward the town square.

"Run!" he shouted. No one listened. Strangely, no one even seemed to hear. He turned and looked back at where the house once stood. A smoking crater had taken its place. The straw-haired boy stepped over a smoldering beam and happily pulled his cart over it, the U-shaped fruits bumping and bouncing as the wheels rolled over the foot-wide plank. He continued to whistle that infernal song.

"Good day!" the boy said as the more-confused-than-ever Ryan stood in shock.

"My house—well, that house, anyway—it was just destroyed by a meteorite!" Ryan cried.

The boy smiled, tilting his head slightly, looking at Ryan as though he were a curiosity in a museum. "What's a meteorite?"

"It's a big rock from space."

"What's space?"

"It's . . . well, it's space. Empty space. Everything up there"—Ryan pointed at the unfamiliar sky—"well, I think it's up there. I guess I'm not sure in this world. But it's really big. Big and black. The stars are up there. They're all trillions of miles apart."

"That sounds made-up."

"Well, it doesn't matter right now," Ryan said, rolling his eyes. "Look over there! My house! Err—somebody's house. There's a flaming hole where it stood just moments ago! My clothes are still charred! My hair is singed!"

The boy looked at the crater. Or rather, through it, as though he didn't see it at all. He looked Ryan up and down, a look of caution. "You're weird," he said. Backing away, he turned and resumed his happy gait, whistling the chorus to "Imagine."

"What's wrong with this place?" Ryan mumbled, feeling his singed hair. He looked like a mad scientist who'd just blown some stuff up in colored test tubes. An orange bird with a long black tail alighted on a twisted piece of molten metal where his home once stood, chirping cheerily. The bird appeared to be whistling "Imagine."

Ryan cleaned out his ears. Maybe he'd hit his head harder than he thought.

The sun fell toward the horizon as Ryan wandered the city in a daze. Well, it may have been a city in this world, but in Ryan's, it would have been considered little more than a roadside stop. A hundred stone homes with thatched roofs were scattered about the side of a gentle green slope that cut its way down toward the seaside cliffs. A narrow dirt road bisected the town, leading away from the sea and into the forest and hills beyond.

He'd stopped several other villagers to tell them what had happened and warn them that worse things might be coming their way sometime soon. They all laughed at him or pretended not to hear him. It was as if the townspeople were under some spell that prevented them from seeing. Or else, perhaps, they didn't want to see.

Most bizarrely, his house wasn't the only one that had been destroyed that day. He counted no less than six other flaming rocks from space that smashed homes, obliterating them and anyone inside them completely. One such disaster occurred not twenty feet in front of him, others further off. Fire from the heavens was raining down on the whole town. Slowly, surely, it would be entirely destroyed sooner or later. And nobody seemed to care.

Ryan had also come across dozens of other craters, cool and weathered from age. Some had new grass growing where the buildings had stood, with stones littering them like gravestones and jagged, rotting wooden beams stabbing upward like skeletal fingers. To any sane person, they would stand as warnings of the dangers of putting your roots down in this doomed place. But the people of the City of Destruction saw right through them.

Ryan finally arrived at the cliffs. They dropped a hundred feet to the ocean below, now crashing against the rocky wall at high tide. He sat down, his feet dangling over the treacherous drop, and watched as the sun dipped below the horizon. Twin moons rose off to his left, one a greenish blue and the other pure white.

"OK," Ryan said aloud. "Think, Ryan. Think."

He began rattling off what he knew, counting off the facts one by one, as though to assure himself they were true.

"I'm Ryan Fleming, and I'm from the San Fernando Valley." He held up one finger.

Saying the words made him feel better. It made this place feel more like a dream and called his own world into crystal-clear focus. Like a camera lens picking and choosing what to focus on, his mind seemed to oscillate between a certainty that his other world was real and this place a foggy dream, and vice versa.

He held up a second finger. "I visited . . . a church . . . this morning. Its name had something to do with fire. Inferno? Ignite? Something like that. But I know that to be true."

He extended a third finger, gaining momentum and confidence.

"The pastor called me up on the stage. I think I challenged him or something. And . . . and . . . that's it. That's all I remember."

He slumped over, defeated. He was no closer to discovering what had really happened—or which world was truly the dream.

Just then, he noticed a huge shape like a shadow lumbering under the surface of the water below the cliffs. It must have been three hundred feet long. He shuddered, realizing how alone and vulnerable he was out here in this strange land or other world—and thinking about how he had been floating, helpless and unconscious, in those eldritch waves.

"Hello there!"

Ryan jumped in fright and whirled around, nearly tumbling off the cliff to the jagged rocks below. He swung out an arm instinctively, slapping whoever it was across the face.

The figure—a man, it seemed—stepped back slightly. He was smiling, wide and bright. He wore what Ryan presumed to be fine clothes for this world: purples and greens and blues with golden thread and matching golden hair. He stood lanky and tall, towering above Ryan by a full foot. Half his face was covered in shadows from the wind-whipped trees above.

"Hello there!" he repeated, having apparently not noticed the blow to his face. "Welcome to the City of Destruction! I'm the Mayor! My apologies for not greeting you earlier. I've had some . . . business to take care of. Very busy lately! Hustle and bustle! Can't stop working! Much to be done!"

He smiled again.

Ryan stepped away from the cliff, glancing behind him. "You know, your town's kinda messed up," he said.

"Haha. I do appreciate humor so," replied the Mayor. "We love humor in the City of Destruction!"

"Yeah . . . about that," Ryan said. "Your town seems to have some kind of fire and brimstone issue. My house—well, I think it's my house—was flattened this morning. I barely made it out alive!"

"Hustle and bustle!" the Mayor said, seeming not to have heard him. "Now, let's get you settled in. A new home for a new you! I have a lovely cottage with full ocean views, and far away from the stenches of the swamp."

"This place is nuts," Ryan muttered. "Yeah, OK. Fine. Just as long as this one's not going to get pancaked again."

"Oh, we have fantastic pancakes in the City of Destruction!" the Mayor said, smiling, as he led Ryan back toward the village.

"Does the fact that your town is literally called the City of Destruction ever give you pause?" Ryan asked, falling in next to the Mayor. "Like, doesn't that ever worry you?'

"We have the finest entertainment in all the Dying Lands," the Mayor said, skipping along.

"My goodness," Ryan muttered. "So your town is called the City of Destruction, and your country—or whatever it is—is named the *Dying Lands*? And that doesn't make you sit back and think about your life a bit?"

"Life is wonderful here, indeed," said the Mayor, not skipping a beat. "Come on out to the town square tomorrow. We are having our annual Festival of Destruction! It will be our most explosive one yet!" He smiled, that python-like grin. "Ah, here we are."

They had come up to the edge of town. A hovel sat inside a wide yard enclosed by a two-beamed wooden fence. The Mayor produced a key and opened the gate that led to the front walk. "Some of our finest housing."

The building was older and more overgrown than his last dwelling—a simple, square building with a sagging roof and weathered stone walls.

"Looks like it's, uh, well-loved," Ryan said. "Pre-owned housing."

"Ah, yes, well . . . the last owners . . . are no longer with us. They were not worthy of the City of Destruction." A sharp and terrible look flashed in the Mayor's eyes, disappearing as quickly as it came. He smiled. "You're going to love it here. You'll forget your old worries, your old life, your old . . . well, you'll see." The Mayor handed him a key.

"Enjoy your rest, Christian," the Mayor said.

"Hey, that's not my . . ." Ryan began, but the words died in his mouth. "Thanks. I will."

"See you tomorrow! The festival begins at dawn!"

The house had two rooms: a main chamber with a fireplace, wooden table and chairs, and a room with two straw beds pushed together. Square windows were cut into the wall. Crude wood panels had been hammered over each of them to keep out the wind and rain. Still, the sea breeze whipped right through them now that the cold of night had overtaken the village.

After some difficulty learning how to use the flint on the mantle, Ryan built a small fire. A modest helping of bread and cheese sat in a small wooden trunk in the front room. Still fresh. Ryan assumed the Mayor had left it. He ate by the fire and then retired, not realizing how exhausted he was. He lay down on the bed and started up again when his back rested on something sharp and hard.

"Ow," he mumbled to himself. A rectangular object was wedged under the off-white sheet. He got up and fumbled around under the blanket, looking for the culprit. "Here we go—what's this?"

It was a well-worn book with a red leather cover. He opened the pages, and his breath caught in his throat. It was written in a strange runic language, but he was amazed to find he could understand it. He read it as though he had been reading it his whole life. It was as if he had been learning this secret language subliminally since he was small, preparing him for this moment, the Book activating his latent fluency.[10]

THE BOOK

On the front page was scrawled the name "Christian"—probably written by the previous owner.

"Whoa," Ryan said. "Aren't I Christian? No, wait . . . I'm Ryan. RYAN."

He flipped through the Book. It was written beautifully, though its words were archaic at times. No, that's not quite right. "Archaic" implies the language related to time in some way. It read as though it had been written outside of time altogether.[11]

The Book spoke of a place called the Golden City. It was, apparently, a fabled fortress of peace that sat on the edge of the Dying Lands, at the end of a long stretch of road built by the King himself. The Road ran through a bubbling bog, a dark forest, and up a lofty peak. The peak was described as a majestic mountain on which sat a wooden cross. Ryan was suddenly filled with a longing to go there, but he did

---

[10] Spoiler alert: this is exactly what happened. Codes were sent to Ryan in his previous life: a baseball card. Droning words from a schoolteacher. Flashing lights in a seizure-inducing episode of *Pokémon*. The Orchestrater of All Things likes to have fun with this kind of stuff.

[11] In fact, it had been.

not know why. Mixed feelings of guilt, shame, and hope filled him as he read about the mystery of this cross.

Ryan sat, enchanted by the words on the pages. There were stories—stories I wish I could tell you people from Earth. Stories of tragedy, stories of love and loss, stories of hope and sacrifice and the triumph of good and evil. The stories were all true, good, and beautiful.

Much of the Book, though, was just general advice for living in the Dying Lands. Some of these proverbs were plain and simple:

> *Do not argue with those who think they are tolerant; they will probably beat your brains out with a shovel.*
> *The one who has Faith has everything.*
> *Always pet a cat when you see one in the street.*
> *Sometimes, all you can do is go forward.*

Others were more cryptic:

> *Bread and cheese are good, but not when a meteor is about to squish you.*
> *Don't eat the purple fruit.*
> *Beware the Smiling Preacher.*

The words enchanted him, even the ones he didn't understand. Maybe especially the ones he didn't understand. Ryan tore through page after page, having forgotten his weariness. He learned of the Dying Lands and something called the Hollowplague: a kind of darkness that consumed town after town across the countryside, making people go insane and destroy each other. And—Ryan shuddered at this part—it made people slowly turn translucent, then nearly invisible, hollowed-out husks of the people they had been before. It started at their toes and fingertips, then moved gradually up their arms and legs and bodies until it consumed their hearts. It wasn't clear how people contracted the Hollowplague—whether it was through contact or airborne or just something that came upon you for no reason at all—but it was clear that it was a horrible way to die. He read of the King's Road: once a stunning highway paved with gold that cut across the land, allowing travel and commerce to flourish. Later chapters in the book said it was in disrepair now, overgrown with weeds. No more than a narrow road that few traveled on these days. Then he read these cryptic words:

The land is dying, the travelers are few.
Follow the road, reach the city.
Ring the bell, wake the King.
Heal the hollow, restore the land.
This is why you were brought through the gateway,
Where the blind dance among the craters.

The Book warned that many would one day believe this "King" to be a myth and would mock those who traveled on his Road. In fact, toward the end of the Book, accounts were given of those who believed the Golden City itself to be a fairy tale, made up by those who needed some kind of false hope to get through their pathetic lives.

And there will come a day when many will turn their backs on the Golden City, calling it a myth and a legend. They will smile at their own destruction. They will grow fat and happy even as their doom draws nigh. They will behold the Golden City on the horizon, and still they will deny its existence, for they love themselves too much.

Ryan looked up, startled to see that the sun was rising beyond his square window. He had read all night. He glanced down at the final page of the Book and breathed in sharply.

Before him lay a drawing of the very home he sat in. It was a detailed sketch done in pencil. Every item was there: the fence, the walkway, the square windows, the lovingly-laid gray stones. But two things about the picture unsettled him deeply: a man sat in the window. A young man—about his age—reading a book. It was him, he was sure of it. The city was sketched into the background.

The other unsettling detail was the giant meteor heading directly for the town.

Ryan ran outside and looked up to the morning sky: sure enough, a huge space rock lit up with crimson fire was sailing directly toward him and the rest of the town. This one would be the end of them all.

He turned to run for the cliffs, the quickest way out of the meteor's path. He hesitated. The townspeople! They'd be killed! Did he care? Weren't these people all just part of a dream anyway? Ryan was no longer so sure. Every moment he spent in this place made it feel more real.

After a moment's struggle, he changed direction and ran toward the town square of the City of Destruction, the shadow on the ground spelling out its doom growing larger by the second.

CHAPTER 4:

CHEESE, ALE, AND METEORS

But you can't make people listen. They have to come round in their own time, wondering what happened and why the world blew up around them.

—Ray Bradbury, *Fahrenheit 451*

Poets have been mysteriously silent on the subject of cheese.

—G. K. Chesterton, "Cheese"

"Meteor!" Ryan screamed as he ran toward the center of town.

Festive banners decorated every street. Flags flew gaily in the breeze. Music floated through the air. Jugglers juggled, kids ran in circles playing at their games, adults drank and ate and laughed. And still their destruction raced nearer.

"Everyone! Meteor!" he cried. He ran through a carnival tent full of tables and chairs with a crowd milling about, everyone happily and obliviously eating bread and cheese and drinking ale.

"We've got to get out of here! Now!" Ryan pleaded.

The people smiled at him. "Would you like some bread and cheese? It's quite good," said one plump serving wench, extending a large plate of the stuff.

It's a fact that humans can easily ignore imminent destruction if there's good bread and cheese to be had. The people of the City of Destruction were no exception. I don't know what it is about cheese, but humans go nuts for the stuff. If I were suddenly granted the ability to taste corporeal food, I'd make a beeline for the bread and cheese. There's something about it: every piece of bread and every kind of cheese is slightly different. It's not like crackers or chips, manufactured in safe little squares, every bite the same. *Sigh.*

Anyway, in spite of his desperate plight, Ryan was tempted to have a piece of cheese, just for a moment. *I'm hungry,* he suddenly thought, *and the meteor can wait. Yes, the meteor is important. But I have plenty of time.* He reached toward the cheese. The wench smiled wider and wider as his hand approached the delicious, buttery yellow piece of sharp cheddar-y goodness. Images of death and destruction faded from his mind. They were replaced with images of pleasure, a full belly, and satisfaction. *I could settle down here,* he thought. *Make this home. I could stay here forever, really.*

The scent of the cheese wafted up through Ryan's nostrils, intoxicating his brain, some dark magic working its way through the deepest parts of his mind. Many great evils have been committed in the world because men were hungry.

No, I whispered in his ear.

Yep, me! The Narrator himself! I was granted permission to intervene at this point, to keep the story on course. The Great Storyteller lets us do this from time to time. *Ryan! Get away from the cheese! Yes, it does look delicious, and boy does it smell good. Mmmm, I'd love to taste chee—NO! WAIT! WHAT AM I SAYING!?! RYAN! THE METEOR!*

"Who's . . . Ryan?" Ryan muttered. He picked up a piece of cheese and brought it to his mouth. "No Ryan . . . only cheese . . . delicious, soft cheese . . ."

Just then, Ryan was jostled by some unseen force[12] and dropped the cheese. It bounced on the ground, its delicious beauty ruined by dirt and grime. Such a sad waste, but it had to be done.

---

[12] Me again! I pushed him! Don't worry, it was an authorized intervention. I have the appropriate Divine Intervention Request forms all filled out and approved right here.

"No! What am I doing? The meteor!" Ryan turned and ran, shoving pub patrons out of the way as he burst outside and dashed toward the town square.

The Mayor was standing up on a wide wooden platform, flanked by musicians, acrobats, fire-swallowers, and even a small elephant.

"Mr. Mayor, you've got to get everyone out of this town!"

Ryan shouted, then tried to catch his breath.

"Eh? What was that?" the Mayor replied, smiling.

Ryan pointed up. "You're . . . all . . . going . . . to . . . die! Let's go!"

The Mayor looked up. "Yes, indeed! Lovely weather we're having! Not a cloud in the sky!"

"You psycho!" Ryan shouted. Pushed past his breaking point, he jumped up on the stage and grabbed a brass bullhorn-like device held by a member of the Mayor's entourage.

"Everyone, please listen to me!" Ryan yelled.

The town quieted down, the revelers looking rather annoyed at this disturbance. The minstrels stopped playing. Everyone looked on curiously.

"There is an asteroid—I mean, a big rock! Yes, a big rock! It's heading for your town right now! You probably have less than a minute if you want to live! Now, if we hurry, we can make it out alive! All you have to do is open your eyes!"

There was a beat of silence. Then laughter. Teary-eyed, raucous laughter. "This guy's the best jester you've hired for Festival yet, Mayor!" said one bard, wiping tears from his face.

"Yes, he's quite . . . charming," the Mayor said, smiling. That dangerous gleam again.

"If you won't believe me, believe this Book!" Ryan shouted, pulling out the old Book and holding it in front of him like a crucifix toward a wilting vampire.

"Where did you find that, boy?" the Mayor said, shrinking back. "Give that here!"

At that moment, smaller rocks from the asteroid above began to pepper the townspeople. Some were bruised. Some were bloodied. Flaming rocks lit several homes on fire. Soon, there was fire all around. But the people went right on partying.

Ryan put the Book back in his pocket. The Mayor's hair caught fire as a flaming piece of rock broke off the asteroid and nearly flattened him.

"Your hair is on fire!" Ryan cried. "Do you believe me now?"

"We are safe and happy!" the Mayor screamed. "THERE IS NO SUCH THING AS JUDGMENT! THERE IS NO SUCH THING AS DEATH! STOP BEING SUCH A TROUBLEMAKER!" The fire then consumed him, melting his face like the Nazi who opened the Ark of the Covenant,[13] even as he continued to scream that there was no meteor.

Ryan jumped off the stage and ran—away from the cliffs, away from the town square, away from the City of Destruction and toward the tree line at the northeast side of town.

He was nearly clear of the city limits, the sounds of the party fading into silence, when he heard another voice: "Wait!"

He turned and saw its source: a man of no more than twenty, lean and fit, with long, dark brown hair flying behind him as he jogged up toward Ryan. "I heard what you said back there, and I believe you."

"You do?" Ryan said.

"Yes. I even started to see glimpses of what you were talking about: the craters, the flaming rocks from the heavens, the big one about to hit us. I didn't see them clearly, mind you, but I saw . . . glimpses. And then I remembered!"

"Remembered what?" Ryan was confused.

---

[13] Another film reference from your world. I am trying to be as relatable as possible here.

"I was brought here too . . . a long time ago. And I found a Book as well. It told me my mission was to ring a bell and awaken a King, I think? Something about saving the world and stuff. I can't quite remember. I really got caught up in the bread-and-cheese scene around here. It's simply exquisite!"

Ryan sighed wistfully. "It really is."

"Anyway, when you arrived and started yelling at everyone about the Book, I came to my senses!"

"Well, I'm glad someone here has some sense," Ryan said. "Welcome to my . . . quest, I guess?"

"The name's Radical," the man said, extending his hand.

"Ryan." They shook.

After a minute or two, they arrived at the hill on the far side of town. The scattered trees drew closer. A fence surrounded the city, with a narrow gate leading out and toward the wilds beyond. "Here we go—through the gate, I suppose," Ryan said.

Suddenly, they heard the sound of rock hitting ground.

Out of breath, they turned, facing the town behind them. They watched in quiet horror as the asteroid hit. It slammed into the earth with incredible speed and force, sending a shockwave through the trees all around. Ryan and Radical were pushed onto their backs. They shielded their faces from the blistering heat.

The City of Destruction was no more. They sat in silence for a few minutes, absorbing the shock of the massive loss of life they'd just witnessed. Then, without a word, they arose and walked quietly through the gate and out onto the King's Road.

"You OK?" Radical asked as they walked under the cool shade of the trees.

"Not really," Ryan said. "I didn't know many of them, but . . . well, I don't handle death very well."

Radical nodded and took a bite of an apple he'd plucked from a tree. "Well, don't feel too bad about them. They were pretty stubborn, after all."

Ryan thought about that for a moment. "Well, yes. But it's still terrible that they've died."

"Oh, yes, yes, terrible. Don't get me wrong. But, I mean, we ought to put that behind us. We made the right choice. That's something to be proud of, isn't it?"

"Well, I don't really think so. I didn't choose any of this," Ryan said thoughtfully. "It was dumb luck that I avoided the first meteorite. And it was dumb luck that I found the Book and narrowly escaped the town, and . . . I wasn't really smarter than any of those poor people. I just happened to make it out, and they didn't. I don't know why my eyes were opened and theirs were not."

"Oh, yes, don't misunderstand, of course," Radical said, holding his free hand up defensively. "But you and I . . . it seems we've got the stuff to go the distance. We can follow this road all the way to the Golden City. It's exciting, in a way."

"Sure, I guess," Ryan said, not feeling excited at all. "So what . . . this must be the King's Road I read about in the Book? And it leads to some mythical city of gold?"

"That's right," Radical said. "The prophecies all say a pilgrim will make the journey, ring the bell, and awaken the King, who will save the land from destruction and cure those inflicted with the Hollow-plague once and for all."

"That all sounds awfully tidy," Ryan said. "Like a bad fantasy novel."[14]

---

[14] Hey, don't blame me! I only write down what I'm told. Besides, who says a great story can't have a simple premise? The premise of life is simple. It's the characters who always manage to confound me. Whether I'm telling the story of a lizard

Radical laughed, and they walked in silence for a while. Ryan did not say so, but he didn't care too much about the plight of the people of this land by that point; he mostly just hoped that completing this bizarre "quest" would somehow end this nightmare and get him home.

They walked along the overgrown road as the sun began to set, carefully stepping over broken stones and upturned bricks. As the shadows grew longer, they began to stumble and their progress slowed. Soon, the light from the sun was gone. Even the smoldering orange glow of the burning city behind them faded away and the light gave way to an eerie blue twilight.

Still, Radical's tone was optimistic as they talked about all the heroic things they would accomplish on their journey.

"Well, isn't this an adventure! We're going to do great things for the King! Way more than anyone else ever has!"

Poooоick. Just then, Radical's foot stuck in something soft and deep. "Hullo, what's this?"

Unable to stop himself in time, Ryan had stepped in it, too. "Ugh. It's a swamp."

They looked up. As far as they could see, a dark, murky swamp stretched ahead and beside. A low fog rolled in. Croaks and chirps grew louder. Ryan thought he could see yellow eyes protruding from the surface of the muddy slop. The roots of massive trees arched up out of the water like monstrous claws.

The pair stepped back and tried to wipe the muck off their shoes.

"Well, so much for a great adventure," said Ryan. "How on earth are we going to get across this?"

"What's earth?" Radical asked.

"It's my planet. Well, I think so, anyway."

"What's a planet?"

---

creature from Universe #DE-377 or a Yeti from Universe #F-437, all universes are united by the truth of one Creator.

"It's a big ball in space."

"What's space?"

"You know what? Never mind. We just have to figure out a way to get across this swamp. I don't know if all this Golden City talk is true or not. But I have a feeling that if I can make it there, I'll finally be able to go home."

They sat on the bank and thought through their predicament. They could try to leave the Road, but that seemed inadvisable. A proverb from the Book read, "*Don't leave the Road, dummy.*" So that option was probably out. Besides, they didn't know just how wide this bog was. They could end up miles off course and have no way of getting back to the Road.

"I've got an idea," Radical said at length. He pulled a long knife from his belt and clambered up one of the swamp-trees. A minute later, a long vine came coiling down from the branches above. "It's a makeshift rope," he said after climbing back down.

"How does that help us, exactly?" asked Ryan as he slapped a mosquito-type insect off his neck.

"Look. We'll each tie an end around our waists. That way, if one of us starts to sink, the other one can help him."

Ryan brightened a bit. "*A vine of two is stronger than a vine of one*," he recited, a passage from the Book.

"Yeah, yeah, exactly. Come on. We're off! For the King!"

"For the King!" Ryan said, feeling kind of foolish but somehow a bit excited by the quest anyway.

They set off again. It was hard going. The vine helped give them peace of mind, but it didn't help with the pilgrims' progress. The mosquitoes came in hard and fast, greedily feasting on them. Dark, slithery Things slipped by their ankles and grumbled under the putrid brown surface.

Radical grew quiet. A word of complaint escaped his lips here and there. Then a curse word slipped out. He began to curse the bog, the mosquitoes, the vine that held them together, the Road, the Book, and the Golden City itself. The change was swift and shocking.

"You know, the City of Destruction wasn't so bad," Radical mumbled.

"It's a giant smoking crater," Ryan replied.

"Yeah, but there weren't any mosquitoes."

"Well, that's true."

They plodded on in silence, the sullen Radical falling further and further back until he finally began to tug Ryan backwards. "I thought this would have a lot more adventure and excitement. I wanted to slay dragons for the King and rescue princesses and besiege castles!" he yelled. "Not walk through a bog!"[15]

"Hmph . . ." Ryan grunted, trying to focus on taking one step at a time without falling.

Radical whined. "I didn't sign up for this!"

"Look, Radical—there's the other bank!" Ryan said happily. Sure enough, not fifty feet from them, a green embankment sloped up and away from the accursed swamp.

"Finally," Radical muttered.

"All we've got to do is get over this log here and—AHH!" Ryan shouted, for at that very moment, he stepped into a sinkhole. Gravity took him, trapping him up to his chest in the black muck.

"The vine! You can pull me out!" Ryan said, struggling to claw his way out of the bog but only sinking deeper with every movement. He looked up at Radical, only to see his faithful companion cutting the vine that connected them with his knife. "Radical! What are you doing?!"

[15] As it turns out, following the King in the Dying Lands and worlds elsewhere often involves the drudgery of walking through a nasty bog. Many travelers dream of doing great, heroic things but are weeded out by drudgery and discomfort. Radical didn't even know how fortunate he was, as the bog on the Planet Dalkel in Universe #FF-237 is filled with man-eating electric squid.

"I told you we shouldn't have left the city," Radical said as he hacked off the final tendrils that bound them together. "You'll probably just drag me down with you in there. No thank you! I'm going back to the City of Destruction. They have excellent bread and cheese."[16]

"Radical, you . . . you traitor!"

"Yes, well, I've had quite enough. I signed up for glory and adventure and all I got was hard work. I hope you find your way to the Golden City, friend! Farewell!"

And just like that, Radical was gone.[17]

Ryan considered his predicament. He had half a vine rope tied around his waist, but nothing to attach it to. He looked around: not a stump, not a rock in sight. There was the log he'd just climbed over, but it was a good ten feet away—far longer than his vine rope.

"OK, stay calm," he said aloud to no one in particular. "The more you move, the more you sink. So just don't move. This is fine. This is all fine."

It was, of course, not fine. Ryan was trapped in the Dying Lands' world-famous Blackmuck. If you've ever seen one of those human movies with quicksand, it's kinda like that. Except Blackmuck is alive. It senses travelers and tries to murder them. At that very moment, the sentience of the sprawling Blackmuck that covered Depression Bog was alerted to Ryan's presence and was spending all its strength and energy to drag him under. Luckily, Blackmuck is pretty slow. It's pretty much just mud, after all—mud that wants to murder you, but mud nonetheless. And mud isn't known for its speed. So Ryan had a little time. But not much.

Suddenly, a sound cut through the creaks and croaks of the bog. It sounded like a car. It was, in fact, a car. Technology in the Dying

---

[16] Radical was mistaken here. The City of Destruction *used* to have excellent bread and cheese. At that moment, all its bread and cheese was quite overcooked.

[17] In case you're wondering, Radical was mauled to death by the Hollow Ones seventeen minutes later.

Lands wasn't as advanced as that in your world, but some clever alchemists and magicians had invented a kind of motor-propelled vehicle—much like your human cars in the early 1900s—at great expense. It was made of pure gold and driven by the richest inhabitant of the country.

And it was this motorcar that Ryan heard driving along the far bank of the bog.

"Help!" Ryan screamed as he saw the strange contraption come rolling into view. "HELP!"

The golden motorcar came screeching to a stop. Out stepped a man dressed in what looked like a modern business suit, which was made entirely of gold. His dark hair was slicked back. His teeth were impossibly white.

"Happy morning to you, sir!" the man cried out, waving.

"No, not happy morning!" Ryan replied. The mud was up to his neck. He could hear it humming and murmuring and bubbling all around him, as though it were alive (once again, it was). "I'm sinking and I need someone to save me!"

The man laughed. "Again, I say, happy morning to you! I'm the Smiling Preacher!" he said cheerily. "You don't need someone to save you! The King has given you everything you need, right here." The preacher tapped his finger against his chest. "You just need to claim victory over your problems!"

"What? Just get over here and pull me out!" Ryan said as the muck continued to rise. "Quick!"

"Oh, you poor thing," the Preacher said. "Your problem, you see, is that you keep speaking your problem into existence. You only need to declare that you're not in a swamp, and you'll be saved. Your words have the power to change your situation! Don't claim anything less than the King's best for you!"

Ryan spat out muck as its oozy, and most definitely alive, tendrils began to slide into his mouth.

"Enough with the crazy talk! You're nuts! Help!"

The Smiling Preacher took a step back. He pulled out a spotless silk handkerchief and wiped a fleck of mud off his expensive-looking shoes.

"Now, listen, son. I don't appreciate you speaking negativity like that into my life."

"HELP!" Ryan's mouth sank beneath the broiling surface. "HLPH!"

"If you don't reach out and claim victory over your problems, well, I can't help you. You need to pick yourself up by your bootstraps."

Ryan just burbled, again, probably trying to call out for help.

"Pathetic," the Smiling Preacher sneered. "Well, have a nice life! If you decide you want my advice after all, I'm just up the road in the golden mansion. It's off the King's Road a ways, but my house is finer than the Golden City itself. Stop in and stay a while if you make it out alive! May the King bless you!"

And with that, the Smiling Preacher jumped into his motorcar and sped off, smiling all the while.

Blackness overtook Ryan. He heard diabolical whispers and ghoulish groans all around him.

"This is your fault."

"You're not good enough."

"The King didn't want you anyway."

"You're not worthy of the Golden City."

Ryan gave up and surrendered his body to Depression Bog. The Blackmuck had claimed another victim. Ryan was one of thousands, another casualty of its wicked reach. He died. And that's the end of the story.

OR IS IT? Did you see what I did there? I made you think it was over, but it isn't! This is called a plot twist. Or a fake-out? I don't know exactly. I'm still studying human narratives, remember? Did I go too far?

Anyway, Ryan *almost* died. But that's when Faith found him.

CHAPTER 5:

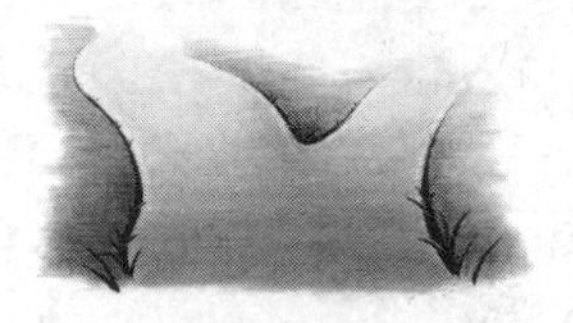

FAITH

Faith is different from proof; the latter is human, the former is a Gift from God.

—Blaise Pascal

Several minutes before Ryan came closer to death than he ever had before, a red-haired, green-eyed woman about his age was walking along the Road, gathering berries and whistling. She heard the noises of a struggle, some shouting, and the sound of a strange growling machine making its way through the woods. She'd watched from behind a tree as the Smiling Preacher gave his helpful advice to Ryan. She'd seen him around before. She'd even saved a few pilgrims like Ryan from him before. The guy gave her the creeps. Anyone with teeth that white had to be up to no good.

Once he was safely out of view, she ran out into the bog, nimbly hopping along rocks and the surface of the swamp. Just as the severed end of the vine attached to Ryan's waist slipped under the mud, she darted out and snagged it, pulling with all her might. Eventually, Ryan's nearly lifeless body started to budge, coming up inch by inch.

Finally, his eyes appeared. Then his nose. Then his mouth. He sputtered and spit and gasped for air.

"Here, grab on!" she said as she reached out to pull him from the surface.

Several minutes later, still short of breath but out of immediate danger, Ryan lay on the far bank of Depression Bog. He didn't know it, but he'd survived the hazard that claims 87.26 percent of pilgrims' lives, their journeys snuffed out before they even began.

"—and everyone knows you're not to cross the bog alone," the red-haired woman was saying as he finally regained some semblance of awareness.

"What?"

"It's in the Book. Didn't you know? Or don't you have a Book?"

"I have the Book," he managed before rolling to his hands and knees and vomiting out tons of Blackmuck. It squirmed and writhed its way back to the bog, squealing and whispering infernal things all the way. "Ugh."

"Sorry. You need to rest. I'm Faith," the woman said, pulling out her waterskin and offering it to him.

"Thanks," he said as he sipped, trying not to drink too much lest he trigger another round of vomiting. "I'm Christia—Ryan, I think."

She smiled. "You're the new arrival, then?"

"I think so? I don't remember much before yesterday. I was at this church, and then I yelled at the preacher, and . . . that's about all I can remember."

"Pilgrims often travel this way," she said, standing up and stretching her legs. "They come by ones and twos. The twos sometimes make it across the swamp. The ones never do."

"Are you a pilgrim too, then? Are you traveling to the Golden City along the King's Road?"

"Yes," she said, turning toward the northeast. Toward the King. She sighed.

"Wait—you crossed the Bog alone then?"

"I don't live in the City of Destruction," she said. "I live here in the woods. My cottage is just there." She pointed toward the east. "I've always wanted to make the journey myself, but my calling is to help pilgrims. When I saw that heaven-rock coming to destroy the City of Destruction once and for all, well, I knew the time had come. There's not much time left for the Dying Lands. Are you . . . you're not . . . ? Well, never mind."

"What?"

"Do you need a companion?"

Ryan sat up, studying her. "Well, I guess so. I don't know much about this pilgriming stuff. But I haven't had much luck with companions so far. You're not going to leave me, are you?"

She laughed, pure and clear. A defiant laugh. "I'd sooner die than leave a companion behind," she said." Ryan believed her. She reached her hand out. Ryan took it, and she pulled him up. She was stronger than he expected.

"Well, I guess we have a deal then," Ryan said. "But if you leave me, I'm going to leave you a bad review on Yelp."

"On what?"

"It's . . . you know what? I can't remember. Never mind."

"So what's the deal with all the pilgrims?" Ryan and Faith had been walking along the Road for some hours, only having stopped once for a light lunch of berries. Ryan had lost his appetite for cheese for a good long while, but he'd need something more substantial soon. The sun began to set, its crimson light weaving through the trees in the thickening forest.

Faith looked him up and down, biting her lip. "You read the Book, right?"

"Yeah."

"There's a prophecy. It's in the Book of Bunyan, Chapter Five, verse twelve. It says, 'A pilgrim shall come to you across time and space. He will ring the bell and save you from the Plague.'"

"I literally understood none of that."

She laughed. "Pilgrims come through here often. Most of them have foggy memories of other worlds. They seem to . . . materialize, for lack of a better word, in houses in the City of Destruction."

"Huh. A spawn point. A portal," Ryan said. "Like in a video game or something."

Faith continued, ignoring him. "Most of them make for the Golden City, but none have made it far. Some die in the City of Destruction, their house flattened by one of those Heaven Rocks. Many die in the Bog. Some are led off course. They say there's a Deceiver in these woods who—"

Faith stopped, frozen to the spot. "Get down," she whispered. She did not wait for Ryan to comply but grabbed him and shoved him down along the embankment on the Road. She followed suit, lying next to him. They peeked over the edge of the road.

There in the woods, not far off, a hundred ghastly blue lights moved slowly through the forest. As Ryan stared off into the trees, he thought he could see shapes: human and yet not, cruel mockeries of men, drifting endlessly in the fog through a land of dead, twisted branches. They shuffled through the woods silently with neither purpose nor direction. After a few moments, they were gone.

"Hollow Ones," Faith whispered as she gave the all-clear to stand. "Victims of the Plague."

"So these Hollowplague people—they're like, zombies?" Ryan asked.

"What's a zombie?"

"You know, mindless creatures, wandering the lands, looking to eat brains, that kind of stuff?"

"Well, they don't eat brains, but the rest of it sounds about right," she said. "They just kind of roam, empty shells of what they once were. And they hate the living. They won't listen to reason. They'll tear you to shreds. Trust me . . . I've seen it."

They walked without speaking for a few minutes, the hairs on Ryan's neck standing on end as he thought of the roaming horde of nearly invisible ghost-people moaning and stumbling through the woods, looking for their next victim.

It was Faith who broke the silence. "It . . . my family . . . everyone I've known . . . they were taken by the Plague," she said. Ryan felt a pang of empathy. Images of a young man, a teenager, came flooding back to him. He was lying on a bed, dying of a disease, tubes and needles sticking in his arms. Ryan was standing by the bed, crying and cursing God.

"Matthew." he said, gritting his teeth. "My brother."

"He was taken by the Plague? You have a Hollowplague in your world?"

"Something like that," Ryan said. "If the Hollowplague makes people forget who they are and die a painful death in six short months."

"Well, I'm sorry." Faith touched his arm. "I wish we knew why the King allowed the Plague. They say He's powerful enough to end it with a clap or a shout or the blast of a trumpet. And yet we suffer." She shrugged and pulled her hand away. "But still. There must be some reason. We have to have faith."

Ryan laughed. "Everything's really on the nose in your world, isn't it? Is this some kind of bad allegory?"

"I don't know what that means."

Just then, they came to a fork in the Road.

"'Two roads diverged in a yellow wood—'" Ryan muttered.

"'—and sorry I could not travel both, and be one traveler, long I stood, and looked down one as far as I could, To where it bent in the undergrowth,'" Faith finished, smiling.

Ryan stood agape. "That . . . that poem is from my world! It's by . . . Richard Snow? No, Robert . . . Ice? No, it's Robert Frost!"

Faith shook her head. "No, that's quite impossible. It's by Gunther Giantslayer. He is the warrior-poet of old who fought the Giants, forcing them back up onto the plateau above the Cliffs Eternal, forever driving them out of our land, over four hundred years ago."[18]

Ryan shook his head. "Well, maybe I'm misremembering, but I could have sworn that was from Earth."

"Maybe . . . maybe there's some crossover?" she mused as they stood at the fork, contemplating which path to take. The fading light made her face glow dimly yellow. "Like two streams that weave in and out of each other, or a husband and wife. Sometimes you're not sure where one begins and the other ends."

The evening sun cast the scene with a golden glow, and it was not hard to imagine that they were standing in the Robert Frost poem somehow.

"Now, which way to go?" Ryan wondered. He pulled out his copy of the Book and flipped through it, but nothing jumped out at him. Faith knew her Book pretty well and said there was something in there about a fork in the Road, but she couldn't for the life of her remember where.

The path to the left looked pleasant. The orange autumn leaves waved in a light breeze. The faint scent of apples floated through the air. They could hear a brook murmuring in the distance. It looked like a Thomas Kinkade painting—just without the warm, inviting-looking stone cottage.[19]

---

[18] This was true. Gunther Giantslayer was a legend in the Dying Lands. When the King's Road was still well-traveled, you couldn't pass through a town or village without seeing booth after booth manned by merchants selling his branded merchandise. Dolls, official Giantslayer cloaks, even a line of expensive leather footwear.

[19] And 100 percent less neon.

The path to the right was very nearly the same. There was an almost imperceptible difference. The trees were a little more bare. Few sounds penetrated the woods, which closed in tighter around the road. Autumn leaves danced along the path as a sharp breeze blew along its well-trod surface.

Ryan thought for a minute. "That way off to the right looks evil. And it's cold, and all I've got is this old cloak. I have a really good feeling about the left path."

"Hmm," Faith said, furrowing her brow.

"What? What is it?"

"How do you know?"

"I dunno—just a feeling. I'm kinda following my heart here. I was raised on Disney movies, and they were always talking about following your heart. What else are we supposed to do?"

"Disney?"

"Um, like stories that you watch. Like a play."

"Oh. Well, I don't remember anything in the Book about following your heart. There *is* a lot of stuff in there about the way being difficult, though. So maybe the right path is the right choice?"

"Eh—I think I'm going left."

"Alright," Faith said, biting her lip. "I'm sticking with you!" She looked troubled but said nothing more.

Of course, if they'd known their Book better, they would have found the passage in Chapter Seven of the Account of Roads and Ways that clearly says, "Always take the right path, no matter how pleasurable the wrong road may seem."[20]

The way was indeed pleasant for the first few hours of their journey along the left path. Birds chirped as they moved along, making

[20] Sorry if this spoils what's about to happen next. Some of your human authors do this thing called "foreshadowing," and I'm trying to pull it off. But maybe it's too heavy-handed? Leave me a review when you make it into eternity, would you? I'm curious about how well I did here.

good progress in the early evening hours. The road was softer along this branch somehow, feeling more like pillows under their feet than pebbles, dirt, and rocks.

Ryan pulled his cloak tighter as the light faded and the darkness closed in. And in. And in. It got supernaturally dark, unnaturally fast. Faith produced a lantern from her satchel and lit it, but the darkness overpowered the light, beginning to suffocate it.

"Maybe we picked the wrong way after all," Ryan said, peering fearfully into the growing darkness.

Faith's light faded. Ryan looked around frantically, but the light Faith had been holding just a moment ago was suddenly snuffed out.

"Faith!" he cried. "Faith! Your light's gone out!"

No answer.

"Faith!" Ryan shouted again, trying to hide the fear in his voice. His shout did not echo at all, as though the darkness was smothering even the sound of his voice. "Where are you? Faith! Don't leave me!"

He failed to hide the fear in his voice. He began to panic. Enveloped in darkness, with no way to know which way was forward and which way was back, Ryan began to run.

As everyone knows, running in the dark is a very bad idea. This proved to be true in Ryan's case, as he almost immediately ran directly into a tree, cutting a deep gash along his forehead and knocking him to the ground.

Ryan struggled to get up. Hot tears ran down his face in spite of himself. He was trying to be strong, but this was too much. Images flashed across his vision: images of a dying brother. Images of himself, alone in a hospital waiting room. Punching a wall. Screaming at the God who had abandoned him, or more likely, was never there at all. And here he was, universes away and, once again . . . all alone.

He slumped against the tree—at least he thought it was a tree; he couldn't see it—and began to sob. A grown man sobbing isn't very

acceptable in human society, but it happens in secret more often than you'd think. It happens in lonely hotel rooms and in quiet pastors' studies and, of course, in private hospital rooms. To be human, I think, is to suffer, yet humans oddly choose to suffer alone rather than be thought of as weak. And here, in the dark, in the strange world that had become his own in the space of a day, Ryan cried.

Hours passed, and the dark showed no signs of lifting, as is often the case with darkness. Ryan curled up on the cold ground. He may have slept, but more likely just drifted in and out of consciousness as one does when one is too exhausted to sleep.

It could have been a day or a week for all Ryan knew when he saw the light. It was faint, but it was there. A small, orange speck off in the distance. He rubbed his eyes and looked again. Were his eyes deceiving him? No, it was there. For sure.

"Faith!?" Ryan called, but he did not hear his own voice. The darkness swallowed it all. "Faith!" He got up and found he had the strength to walk after all. One foot in front of the other, he walked through the darkness. He walked for what seemed like an hour. The speck was no closer, but it was somehow brighter.

"Is that you? It's Ryan!" He grew frantic and started to run at full speed, throwing caution to the wind. Unbeknownst to him, he narrowly avoided colliding with 157 trees; some divine force prevented him from knocking himself out.

Suddenly, a bursting, brilliant light blinded him. He emerged from the darkness into full daylight.

"Ryan!" Faith stood in front of him, holding her lantern high and defiantly. She leaped toward him and embraced him. He was a pitiful sight, dirty, bloodied, and scared. He hugged her tight.

"You said you wouldn't leave me!"

"I didn't!" Faith said, her eyes round and wet. "The darkness separated us. You were just . . . gone. I wandered for hours with nothing but my light to guide me. It didn't shine much, but it never went out. And then it was like I passed through a curtain. All the darkness was gone!"

Ryan looked around and was shocked to find they were right back where they'd started, looking at the same fork in the road they had looked at however many dark hours, or even days, ago.

Faith smiled. "Well, at least we know which way to take now."

Ryan shook his head and slumped to the ground. "No."

"What? We have to go right. To the left is only darkness and despair."

"I want to go home," he said. "There has to be a way to leave this accursed place and get back to my world." *Accursed?* He thought. *I'm even talking like the people in this bizarre fantasy novel now. Couldn't I at least have landed in a good book like* Lord of the Rings *or something? I've gotta get back to my world!*

"You can't leave us," Faith said. "We have to get to the Golden City. We have to wake the King and save everyone from the Plague. You know the stakes for my world. You know what the Plague can do."

Ryan ignored her. "Is there any other way out? Is there another way for me to get home?"

"Well . . ." she looked away.

"There is!" he said with newfound resolve. "I knew it. I knew you were holding out on me. Is it a spell? An incantation? Some magic dance? Do I click my heels together and say 'There's no place like home'?"

"No. It's not like Oz," she said.

He rolled his eyes. "You know *The Wizard of Oz*? Where the heck[21] am I?"

---

[21] He didn't say "heck." But the Creator wants me to get this story into religious bookstores, and apparently a ton of religious types have a hard time with something they call "the F word."

"Oz was the ruler of this land some fifteen hundred years ago. He created a bunch of metal machines and nearly conquered the known world. He was driven out by a girl in red slippers."

"Look, this is clearly a dream, or I'm dead and this is some kind of *Lost* situation," Ryan said, throwing a rock into the woods. "I just want to get out of here. How? How do I do it? Other pilgrims must have given up. I'll just do what they did. I'm not your chosen one or your Neo or whatever. I'm just a guy from California on some weird acid trip. Maybe the next guy will save you."

She bit her lip, which quivered slightly. She thought for a moment. Finally, she sighed. "We don't have much time left. You saw what happened to the City of Destruction. Soon, the whole world will be covered in stone and fire. We're in the last days here, and time is running out to reverse the Hollowplague and restore the land. I'll die here, you know."

"You're! Not! Real!" Ryan shouted suddenly. "This whole world is a dream. You know that, right? You're in on this! Is this some kind of *Truman Show* scenario? Where are the cameras?! Are they in the trees? HEY, MOM! I'M ON TV!!!" Ryan flapped his arms like a chicken as he screamed at the tree trunks surrounding them.

Faith stared at him, her green eyes wide.

"Stop looking at me like that!" Ryan said. "You're just part of this crazy dream!"

She hesitated. After a moment, she shifted her pack. She retied her shoes.

"What are you doing?" Ryan asked, some of the crazy having gone from his voice.

"I'm going back home to wait for the next pilgrim. If there is a next one."

"What do you mean, 'if there is a next one'?" he said. "You said that the City of Destruction place is like a spawn point."

She shot him a look, and his face fell. "Oh yeah. It's been destroyed, hasn't it? Does that mean I'm the last one?"

She shrugged. "I don't know." She looked into his face. Her eyes were full of fire. "I really do hope you find peace. May the King bless your travels across time and space."

He nodded. "Thanks. And . . . sorry."

"Me too."

And with that, Faith turned and walked back into the sunset, leaving Ryan alone at the crossroads.

CHAPTER 6:

A DEAL WITH THE DEVIL

It's a mess, but that's what you get for listening to Satan.

—Frank J. Fleming, *Hellbender*

Ryan stood at the crossroads alone. The woods seemed to be frozen in an eternal twilight as he debated his path. Back? To where? The City of Destruction, which was now a smoking crater? Forward? Where there was nothing but fear of death, and who knows what beyond?

If only there were a way to go back home, he thought.

"Hello," said a voice.

Ryan whirled around.

"You look like you're wondering if there is a way to go back home," said the figure standing before him. He was clearly a man, yet something in his grey eyes said he was not a man at all. He wore a business suit like the ones from Ryan's own world. Though he stood on the dusty road, there was not a speck of dirt on his shiny black shoes. His head was entirely bald. He wore thin, silvery glasses. The fading sunbeams seemed to miss him entirely, as though he were not really there at all. As though he simply existed beyond the rules of time and space. He did not smile, but he did not glare. He was simply there.

"Well, yeah," Ryan said, his voice betraying some discomfort. "Uh, but who are you?"

"Well, I am the Devil, of course," the figure said.

"Oh," said Ryan. "So I'm probably not supposed to listen to you."

The man shrugged. "You do you, I always say."

He continued to stand, not really looking at Ryan—rather, looking through him.

Ryan shifted uncomfortably.

"So, uh . . . but, you do know a way out of here?"

"Yes."

"What's, uh . . . what's the catch?"

"No catch," said the Devil. "I'm not going to take your soul or make you battle me in a fiddle duel. Unless you want to. It's been a long time since I've had a good fiddle duel. Johnny, his name was. Gave me a real run for my money."[22]

"I don't know how to play the fiddle," Ryan said.

"It's a lost art," said the Devil.

"Yeah, I guess," said Ryan.

They stood in silence. Ryan did not like the way the Devil made him be the one to continue the conversation. The Devil was not a very good socializer. But the way he mentioned the way home . . . it made the words echo in his brain until it nearly drove him mad. He had to know.

"So, this way home," said Ryan. "What is it?"

"Why, it's in your Book, of course," said the Devil. And he quoted:

---

[22] The Devil was referring to his legendary duel with a traveler named Johnny atop an out-of-control starship as it careened toward a black hole. And they weren't so much fiddles as golden fission-powered laser cannons that made music when they fired. When Johnny woke up, his name was Charlie Daniels of Earth and he remembered barely enough of the story to write a catchy song about it. When interviewed about the idea for the song, Daniels said: "I don't know where it came from, but it just did." Now you know.

Worlds apart, yet intertwined
Worlds separated by a stream
Send me down the River of Time
And all this will be as a beam

"It was in the Book all along? And all I have to do is say those words or something? That's it?"

"That's it."

"I don't have to form a circle of stones, sacrifice a goat, or draw a pentagram or anything?"

"You can if you want to. That's pretty old-school, though. We had a lot of fun with that in your world, for a time. Now we just feed your people Netflix shows instead. It's a lot easier. Less of a mess to clean up."

"Uh, thanks, I guess," said Ryan.

"Goodbye," said the Devil, and Ryan was alone again.

"Worlds apart, yet intertwined . . . worlds separated by a stream . . ." he muttered. He took a breath. His chest started to close up, as though reality itself were folding in on him, pressing in all around. The woods started to bend in his direction. "Send me down the . . . River of . . . Time . . ." He started to grow nauseous. The road in front of him bent upward, folding toward him. His legs gave way.

"Ryan!" He heard a voice, and the spell was broken. The world snapped back into reality, firm and whole. Faith stood in front of him, and all was as it had been before.

"What are you doing?!" she cried.

"I was returning home, until you rudely interrupted me," he replied. "I thought you'd left me."

She sighed. "I had a really bad feeling about all this."

"Like in *Star Wars*."

"What?"

"Never mind."

"Where'd you learn that spell?"

"Well, the Devil told me," he said.

"Didn't you think maybe you shouldn't listen to the Devil?"

"Well, yeah, but I wanted to go home."

"He always misquotes the spell, Ryan. He's done this to pilgrims before."

Ryan's heart caught in his throat.

"He read it to me right out of the Book."

"Yeah—but he twists one tiny word at the end. 'All this will be as a beam' should be 'All this will be as a dream.'"

"What—what would have happened if I'd finished it?"

"I'm not entirely sure," she said. "Though I suspect it would have sent you to the wrong place entirely.[23] One time, he tricked this guy Bob into saying it. He warped miles up into the air over the Great Plateau. They had to scrape him off the ground with a broadsword."[24]

Ryan shuddered. "Well, that was a close one. Uh, thanks, I guess."

She nodded.

"But if I say the *real* spell, that takes me home?"

She shrugged. "Probably. I guess so. If it's in the Book, it's true."

"Well. I guess the deal with the devil is going to pay off after all."

"I guess so. Well, good luck," she said. She did not make eye contact, Ryan noticed. He was sad to notice this, and he was also a little mad at himself for being sad.

"What's wrong?" he asked.

"Seriously?" she said, shooting him a look. This time she made full eye contact, with fire and ice. Now he found himself wishing she'd look away again. "You're the millionth pilgrim to come through. We

---

[23] This is more or less correct. The twisted version of the Return Spell as recorded in the Book sends pilgrims to a completely randomized spot in time and space. The Devil has tricked 32,929 pilgrims into saying it so far. Most end up floating through outer space forever. One particularly unlucky guy landed in Portland.

[24] This is only half correct. Half of Bob ended up above the Great Plateau. His other half is currently somewhere near Alpha Centauri.

keep waiting for the one who will make it, the one who will ring the bell and end the Plague. I dunno. I just thought maybe you were the one."

Now it was his turn to look away. "Look, I wish I could help," he said. "But I didn't sign up for any big quest. I'm just broken and messed up and ready to be done here. And I'm still 99 percent sure this is all some bad trip from a rotten church donut."

Faith bit her lip. "I understand. Goodbye." She slung her pack back over her shoulder and turned to go. As she stepped away, her sleeve caught on an overgrown branch creeping over the road.

Ryan gasped. Her arm—from shoulder to fingertips—was shot through with veins of blue. The scars ripping up and down her skin were translucent; he could nearly see through her arm. The Plague, Ryan could see, was inching ever closer to her heart.

She hurriedly covered the tear with her cloak and kept walking.

"How long do you have?" Ryan called after her.

"What do you care?" she shot back, not turning around.

"I'm going to regret this," Ryan muttered. He ran after Faith and grabbed her. Spun her around. "How long have you had the Plague? How long do you think you have?"

"Let go of me," she said, pulling her arm away.

"Is that why you've been so insistent? You don't have much time?"

She looked away from him. "I suppose so. I got the Plague six months ago. It just started for no apparent reason. No one knows what causes it."

"How long, Faith?"

"Weeks, at best. Or months. I don't know. And the land is about to be covered in fire anyway, so what does it really matter?" She wiped a tear from her eye. "It's not that I'm afraid of death. Every man dies. I just hoped I'd be around to see the land reclaimed. To see the King return."

"I'm sorry, Faith."

"Don't be, Christian."

Christian . . .

That name. *Christian*. He had been fighting back that name, desperate to hold on to "Ryan," the name he had always known, from the world he had always known—that pale blue planet in Universe #532-C. But when Faith called him "Christian," whether by accident or fate,[25] something happened. It felt real. It rang true.

Names are pretty powerful things. There's a reason why the Creator actually bothered to name all the stars. It's also why He made such a fuss about renaming humans like Abram, Jacob, and Simon Peter. And it's why *Birds of Prey: And the Fantabulous Emancipation of One Harley Quinn* bombed at the box office. Not to mention *John Carter*. What a waste of a great franchise![26]

Anyway, Ryan, or Christian, or whatever you want to call him, repeated the name again, quietly to himself. *Christian . . . Christian . . .*

It was as if hearing that name from Faith's lips anchored him here in the Dying Lands. This wasn't just a dream. This was real somehow, and he knew it deep in his bones. He looked at the jagged brown pebbles on the path below him. He took a deep breath and smelled the air as if for the first time. The earthy fragrance of the forest filled his nostrils. He looked around at the strange creatures in the trees, then at the far-off mountains, then at the fair-faced, fire-haired girl staring up at him with tears in her eyes.

My name is Christian.

Memories began trickling in from this bizarre alternate personality fighting for control of his body and mind. A name given to him by a king. A failure that filled him with shame. An escape from a doomed city. And finally, the words from a Book. *Sometimes, all you*

---

[25] Which, you might be surprised to know, are often the same thing.

[26] All the events of the *Princess of Mars* series actually happened, you know, in Dimension 872P. Edgar Rice Burroughs visited their version of Mars in a dream several times.

can do is move forward. The words came to his mind—not as a memory of a dying boy named Matthew—but as a memory of reading the Book he still held in his hand, here in this world. He opened the Book to a dog-eared page toward the end and read the words aloud.

"Sometimes, all you can do—"

"—is move forward." Faith completed the sentence as Ryan looked up, his own eyes starting to fill with tears.

Ryan held out a hand to his companion.

"Come on, Faith. Let's go save your world."

CHAPTER 7:

CHESTERTON'S FENCE

There exists in such a case a certain institution or law; let us say, for the sake of simplicity, a fence or gate erected across a road. The more modern type of reformer goes gaily up to it and says, "I don't see the use of this; let us clear it away." To which the more intelligent type of reformer will do well to answer: "If you don't see the use of it, I certainly won't let you clear it away. Go away and think. Then, when you can come back and tell me that you do see the use of it, I may allow you to destroy it."

—G. K. Chesterton, *The Thing*

Demons, I get. People are crazy.

—Dean Winchester, *Supernatural*

Ryan and Faith walked on through the twilight until the darkness was thick around them. They took shelter on the side of the road, being careful not to stray too far, as Faith warned that the Dying Lands had a way of pulling hapless travelers away from the King's Road.

When he awoke in the morning, far too early for his liking, Ryan had a knot in his back to match the knot on the log on which he'd dozed. He rubbed the sleep from his eyes and groaned. His brave decision from the night before now seemed to be foolishness, as brave decisions often do the morning after you make them.

"Good morning!" said an annoyingly chipper Faith as she cooked something that didn't look very appetizing over the fire.

"Squirrel?" Ryan asked warily.

"Bat," she replied.

"I think I'll pass," he groaned.

"Berries, then," she said, tossing him a leather pouch.

They were surprisingly delicious and filling.

The pair got a move on. "You got a little something on your, uh, your chin there," Faith said, suppressing a smile. Ryan reached up and wiped the purple dribble off.

"Thanks," he said. "Wouldn't want any of the goblins or monsters or whatever we're gonna face here to see me in that state."

She laughed. "What's a goblin?"

"They're like, uh, green monsters with clubs," he said.

"Well, there are certainly monsters in this world," she said. "No green ones, but we have a ton of purple ones, and quite a few human ones too."

He chewed on that as they walked. The path slowly bent to the south and began to descend into a valley of green and gold. Far in the distance, they could make out a mountain range of impossibly high peaks jutting up into the tall, majestic clouds.

As far as epic journeys of adventure that will certainly end in death go, it was quite beautiful.

Wait, was that a spoiler?

"Behind me, quick," Faith said suddenly. Ryan stopped in his tracks and stood dumbly on the road, craning his neck to look around her.

She rolled her eyes. "Or just stand there, I guess. You're definitely going to get me killed."

"What is it?" he asked. They'd come to the bottom of the valley. The trees pressed in closer on this part of the road, and it wove through a soft embankment about ten feet high on either side of them.

Without turning, she reached back and guided him to the edge of the road. The pair leaned up against the sloped earth and listened.

Ryan heard shouts and jeers coming from up around the bend.

"People," she said.

"Oh, good. Not monsters."

"I didn't say that," she said.

"Can't we just go around?"

She shook her head firmly. "From the sound of it, they're on the Road," she said. "At least a dozen of them. And the number one rule of traveling on the Road is—"

"You don't talk about traveling on the Road?" Ryan joked. Faith just stared at him.

"You know, from *Fight Club*? Oh yeah, right. I keep forgetting you have no clue what I'm talking about. If you ever visit my world, we're definitely watching *Fight Club*."[27] He looked back in the direction of the voices. "Maybe they're friendly?"

"Just stay with me and let me talk to them," she said.

They got up and slowly crept along the road. As they rounded the bend, the crowd came into view. A group of about twenty stood some ten yards off the road. They faced a long, wooden fence. It surrounded a green field dotted with tall oak trees. Many of the people held protest signs, while others wielded bricks, pitchforks, and torches.

As Ryan and Faith approached, they could make out the chants at last: "Tear it down! Tear it down!" A handful of the protesters had climbed up on the fence and begun rocking it back and forth, trying to topple it down to the ground.

"What are they doing?" asked Ryan.

"I don't know, but I'd rather not find out," Faith said.

---

[27] The *Fight Club* character Tyler Durden did pay a visit to the Dying Lands twelve centuries ago, but he never left the City of Destruction. He gorged himself on cheese until he became really disillusioned with the meaninglessness of it all and burned down the whole city before killing himself. Sad.

"Maybe they won't notice us," Ryan whispered as the duo crept along the far side of the road.

"Hey!" shouted one of the protesters, noticing them.

"Darn."

Faith stood tall and answered. "We're simply passing by. We don't know what quarrel you have with that fence, but we're neither for you nor against you."

"Impossible," the man answered. Other members of the crowd now started breaking away from the pack and approached. Ryan felt his body tense up and his heart beat faster. "We are protesting this fence and intend to tear it down. And those who aren't with us are against us. We're progressive thinkers, see, and if you don't join our revolution, you must be one of the bigoted, hateful people who built this oppressive fence."

"What's the fence for?" Ryan asked as he and Faith tried to edge along the road, their escape path rapidly being closed by approaching protesters.

"What?" asked the leader, narrowing his eyes. "What's that supposed to mean?"

"Why do you hate the fence so much?" Ryan pressed, hoping to distract him in conversation long enough to get away.

"Hey, everyone, this guy's a bigot!" the leader shouted. The whole crowd of rioters now came and encircled them. "He asked why we're tearing the fence down!"

Jeers and boos came from all around them. A brick flew past Faith's head.

"Wait, wait!" Faith shouted, holding her hands up. "Forgive my friend; he's new around here. All he was trying to say"—she chose her words slowly and carefully—"is that this fence very well might need to come down."

The crowd quieted down, listening to her words intently. Hands with bricks were slowly lowered.

"It's quite possible," she continued, "that the fence is all the things you say: oppressive, restrictive, and unnecessary."

Bricks continued to lower.

"But," she added.

Bricks started to be raised.

"But . . . shouldn't we first ask what the fence is for before we just tear it down?"

"Boo!" jeered the crowd. "She's pro-fence!"

"I'm not pro-fence!" she protested. "I didn't even know the fence existed until a few minutes ago!"

Bricks flew. One flew straight for Ryan, and he heard bones snap and crunch as it smashed into his knee.

"Run!" Faith cried.

"I don't think that's gonna happen," he groaned, falling to the ground.

The protesters closed in. "Down with the establishment! Death to all fences!" they shouted as they dropped their bricks in favor of their fists. They grabbed hold of Ryan and Faith and began pummeling them as they desperately tried to shield their faces and bodies from the blows. Boots crunched on their ribs, arms, and legs as they curled up on the dusty road, certain this was the end.[28]

Just then, they heard a loud thud coming from the side of the road. The fence had finally buckled under the weight of the crowd and crashed to the ground in a pile of splintered wood. The crowd stopped and looked up. Then they cheered, seeming to forget all about the traveling companions. "The fence! It's come down!" they cried, running over to revel in their triumph. "We are free! The oppressive systems keeping us down have been dismantled!"

---

[28] This wasn't the end, so don't worry. There is plenty more story to tell. I just got the sense that maybe you were getting worried. So hang in there. Though there is still a major death ahead. So get ready for that. It's a tearjerker.

And that's when they saw the giant two-headed bull heading right for them. Freed from the fence surrounding its field, it charged. Its eyes glowed red, and fire came from its mouth.

Since there might be younger people reading this book, I'll spare you all the gory details of what happened next. I won't describe the intestines ripped out by sharpened horns, the brain matter splattered all over the road, the skulls shattered and spines snapped and ribs cracked clean in two.

And, my goodness, the screams. So many screams.

So instead of telling you all those horrifying details, I'll just say that it was ugly. A few scattered protesters managed to get away, but most of them were roadkill. Completely unidentifiable, really. A total mess.

Faith and Ryan weren't in great shape either. While she had managed to avoid most of the bull's charges through her nimbleness and years of experience traveling the road, Ryan was still a computer programmer at heart and took a few good licks.

The bull's anger was finally satiated, and it slowly trudged back into its field, wandering the rolling green hills in search of someone else to gore.

Faith and Ryan got up and brushed themselves off.

"Ow," said Ryan, nearly collapsing. He leaned on Faith for support.

"Ow," said Faith.

"Ow, indeed!" said a voice. They slowly turned. Off the side of the road, as though he had been watching the whole time, sat a merry fat man on a white rock. Tiny spectacles sat on his round nose, and a full tuft of wavy hair sat atop his head. His enormous gut threatened to be the end of several buttons on his waistcoat. He held a sketchpad in one hand, a piece of white chalk in the other, and a cigar in his mouth. "Wondrous! Utterly wondrous!" he muttered as he drew something on his pad.

"Are you . . . are you one of them?" asked Faith.

"Beg your pardon?" he asked cheerily in a shrill British accent. "You mean the reformers? The ones tearing down the fence? Heavens no! I'm simply a small man out on a great adventure through a wondrous world. One of them, indeed! Ha! I seem to have lost my hat, though. Wind took it."

He went back to his drawing as though Faith and Ryan were not there, whistling as he worked away.

"They're fools, you know," he said suddenly, as though the conversation had never stopped.

"What?" asked Ryan.

"The reformers. Utter fools! Everyone knows one does not tear down a fence unless one knows the purpose for which it was built!"

He went back to his drawing. The three took in the awkward silence. Faith coughed and drew a circle in the dirt with her toe. The man took no notice.

"What are you drawing?" asked Ryan at length.

"Hmm? Oh, I am drawing the most wondrous thing in all of creation." The man did not elaborate.

"Well, I guess we should be going," Faith said more quietly, turning away from the eccentric man. "What a strange person."

"I must be on my way too," the man said, putting his stub of a cigar, which he had smoked with alarming speed, out on the chalky white rock on which he sat. He flicked it away toward the woods.

"Smokey wouldn't like that," Ryan said.

"Who?" Faith asked. "Is this another reference from your world?"

"It was this bear who told us not to start forest fires."

"Bears talk in your world?"

"Well, no. I mean, kind of."

"Here you are, then," the fat man said suddenly.

"What?"

"A gift for you!" he said. He ripped out the page on which he was drawing and held it out. Faith limped over and took it.

"Well, I have things to do. I do believe the survivors from that little debacle are on their way at this very moment to tear down a most important lamppost on the other side of my field. I shall have to defend it. The monk can't do it on his own!"

"Good luck," Ryan called after him.

The man walked merrily through the field, singing as he went, until the melody finally faded into the distance.

Faith handed Ryan the paper. On it, in white chalk, was the simple outline of a daisy.

CHAPTER 8:

HEALTH AND WEALTH

It's just a flesh wound.

—The Black Knight, *Monty Python and the Holy Grail*

Ryan and Faith trudged along the road as the sun moved higher and hotter in the sky. Well, *limped* is more accurate in Ryan's case. I'm no doctor—that's a whole different department up here in eternity—but I can safely say that his leg was in very bad shape.

"Ugggh," Ryan moaned at length. "I can't go on much longer."

"Let me see," Faith said. They stopped in a small ditch to the side of the road, just out of the reach of the sun's brutal beams. She bent and examined the gash on his leg as he sat in the dust. "Ryan! It's really bad!"[29]

Ryan winced. "Thanks. You're supposed to pretend it's not that bad so I don't freak out."

"Oh. Sorry. Well, I can't treat you here. We need to get you to the City of Evangelion."

"What's that? How far is it?"

---

[29] See? I told you.

"It's not far—maybe two days' journey," she said.

"I don't know if I can hold out that long."[30]

Faith bit her lip, fearing he was right. "We'll just have to keep moving."

He sighed and stood and off they went. After some time, they saw a building just off the side of the road to their left. It gleamed in the sun, for it was made of gold inlaid with intricate designs of silver, and no oxidation or grime marred its pristine surface. It sprawled across a large, immaculate lawn surrounded by a golden fence. The windows were stained glass, sending rainbows dancing across the grass.

"We have to stop," Ryan said, wincing from the wound on his leg.

"I don't know," Faith said. "We aren't supposed to leave the road. But that wound . . ."

"It's not off the road," Ryan said, gesturing toward the intricate golden gate that opened right onto the highway.

"Well, I guess that's true," Faith said, but her eyes said she still had her doubts.

The gate was unlocked. It was wide and opened onto a path that seemed to be made of crystal, leading right up to the large double doors of the house.

Faith knocked. The door opened instantly.

"Come in," said a soothing voice from somewhere in the dark behind the door. "You look tired. Come take a rest in the House of Prosperity."[31]

Ryan limped in, his arm around Faith for support. Their eyes adjusted to the relative darkness, and as the grey mist on their eyesight faded, the sight before them took their breath away.

---

[30] Ryan was quite correct on this point. In fact, unbeknownst to him, the two-headed bull that had slashed him was none other than Mordecai, the dreaded possessed bull of the Dying Lands, and there was poison in his horns. He'd claimed the lives of hundreds of travelers, and Ryan was pretty lucky to be alive. If he didn't get treatment within the next seventy-two minutes, he was going to drop dead. Not good!

[31] Your creepy-siren should be going off right about now.

The home was filled with gold coins, treasure, gems—unimaginable riches. There were bags of cold, hard cash.

A man with golden hair and pale skin—smooth, silky, almost pure white—stood wrapped in fine robes before them. His fingers were covered in rings of various shapes and sizes. He smiled and held his arms out wide. "Welcome, travelers. My name is Health-and-Wealth. It pleases me that you have chosen to stop at my humble little cottage."

He glanced down at Ryan's wound.

"Oh! You have been wounded. Well, by the King's providence, you have come to the right place."

"You believe in the King?" Ryan asked. "Why haven't you made for the Golden City yet?"

Health-and-Wealth smiled. "You young pilgrims are always so excitable! A bit naïve, but that's to be expected. Ah, to have that kind of passion again! So adorable. We need more of that in the world. Oh, well, don't you worry about me. I have some affairs to take care of here. I will make my way eventually."

"You haven't got much time left," Ryan responded. "The City of Destruction is gone, and the rest of the land will follow soon, if the prophecies are to be believed. And, you know, the meteors falling from the heavens."

"Shhh, child, shhhh," Health-and-Wealth said. "You need to rest."

"What we need," said Faith, crossing her arms, "is to get a move on. We'll take aid if you're offering it, but we don't have time for rest."

Just then, Ryan collapsed, landing in a pile of gold coins like Scrooge McDuck taking his morning swim.

A concerned look crossed Health-and-Wealth's face. "Please, miss—please. Just let me treat him, let's get him some water and let him rest, and then you can be on your way. You shall see the Golden City in less than three weeks' time from here. With my powers and resources, you'll get there soon and in style."

After a moment's hesitation, Faith reluctantly stepped aside and let Health-and-Wealth pick up Ryan's limp form. He whisked him away to a back room as Faith looked around. She picked up some paper money. It had a drawing of a man in a wig on it. Strange stuff. She dropped it and wiped her hand on her cloak. It looked clean and freshly printed, but it felt filthy.

In the other room, Health-and-Wealth laid Ryan on a soft bed. Intricately carved posts with pulled-back silk curtains surrounded a soft down mattress. "You sleep now, child," he said. Before he left the room, he pulled out a vial of an ointment of some kind and rubbed it on Ryan's leg. He intoned some words in a language I could not understand. The door closed, and Ryan slept, deeply and contentedly.

Outside the window of Ryan's comfortable room, a bald man in a suit stood staring blankly at the sleeping pilgrim. The hint of a smile formed on his lips, and just like that, he vanished.

"Do you like it?"

Faith jumped back from the painting she had been examining on the wall. She whirled around, and there stood Health-and-Wealth, smiling.

"Sorry. I didn't mean to startle you."

"What is it?" she asked, turning warily back to look at the piece of artwork. It was framed in gold. The painting seemed to shift before Faith's very eyes. It first appeared as a painting of the Golden City, faintly in the distance. Then, the paint itself seemed to swirl and move, transitioning into vague shapes and shadows.

"It's magic, as you've no doubt figured out," Health-and-Wealth answered, smiling. "It cost me quite a bit to acquire that painting. To be honest, it's one of the reasons I haven't left yet. It seems like it would be hard to pack it up and carry it all the way to the Golden City. Not to mention all my other possessions!"

He gestured all around him at the bags of money, piles of coins, and stacks of gold, and sighed.

"And that river you have to cross at the end of the journey! My servants would never be able to get my beautiful painting across. There are moving services, of course, but they're expensive. Bother it all. Sometimes I wonder if going to the Golden City is more trouble than it's worth. Bah! If I can't bring all my stuff, then what's the point?"

"What is this showing me? My heart's desire?"

"Exactly," Health-and-Wealth said proudly. "It will change for each person. As you gaze upon it, it shows you what you want."

As Faith gazed upon the painting, it seemed to gaze into her, asking her what she truly wanted. The Golden City kept flashing into view, but then it would disappear again, shrouded in clouds and veiled in mists. As the painting searched her heart, she doubted. Did she really want to reach the Golden City after all? She thought she did, but sometimes she couldn't conjure up an ounce of desire for the place.

Her heart stopped in her throat. There in the painting, depicted in masterful strokes, still throbbing and coursing with energy, was herself. She stood strong and proud, a brave warrior. She was not in the Golden City, but at her home. As she watched, the picture seemed to move, and her parents stepped out of a small cottage behind her. Somehow, the painting came alive, flashing a thousand images into her mind, a full life in the Dying Lands. She was healthy, no infection threatened her. She was wealthy, she had everything she needed. She was content.

"I can give you all this," whispered Health-and-Wealth. She turned and looked at him narrowly. The smile was gone from his face. "You can have it all. Your faith, Faith, activates the King's will for your life. Name what you want, and it is yours." He lifted his hand.

One of his rings shone a bright red. "Your faith will activate the power of the King. Name it. Name it, and it's yours."

Faith looked into his eyes. Her own welled up with tears. As she looked at him, he glanced at the painting, admiring it. She followed his gaze—and then started in horror.

For the briefest moment, the painting had shown an image of Health-and-Wealth. He stood atop a pile of gold. The gold was covered in blood. At the foot of this mountain lay the body of Ryan. His life energy was sucked away, his soul was gone.

He was a Hollow One.

Faith recoiled and stared wide-eyed at Health-and-Wealth. His eyes snapped toward her. The painting faded back to a swirling void of nothing. "What did you see?" he asked, his eyes narrowing.

"Nothing," she lied, inching for the door leading back to the main hall. "I need . . . I need to rest."

"You're a terrible liar," Health-and-Wealth said. "And I would know. I'm the best." He held his hand up, and his ring shone a more brilliant red.[32] "You could have had it all, you know. I really can make all your dreams come true."

"None of this . . . none of this is real," Faith said, backing away a little faster.

Health-and-Wealth gnashed his teeth. "Reality can be whatever I want."

Suddenly, his pale, perfect skin started to melt away like hot wax. He was transformed before her very eyes into a demon—not one of those demons with pitchforks and tails and little goat hooves like you've perhaps seen in Gary Larson cartoons, but rather the real deal.

They're quite hard to describe, if I'm being honest. I've encountered quite a few myself over the years. It's easier, in fact, to describe

[32] Health-and-Wealth had acquired this precious stone at great personal risk and cost on an interdimensional trip of his own.

how a demon *feels*. Think of a time when you've lost something precious: a child, a spouse, a parent, a sibling. Now think of a time you've felt the full weight of the guilt of sin crushing down on you. Now put that in a vaguely humanoid shape. That's what a demon "looks" like. They aren't really a specific color, not red or black or grey—they're *absence*. The absence of light, hope, and joy. They are the void itself.

So you can understand why Faith's knees buckled when she saw Health-and-Wealth's true form. You can understand why her strength left her and she fell to the ground. And you can understand why she'd think this was the end as Health-and-Wealth gleefully lunged for her, ready to suck out her soul, as he'd taken the souls of so many before.[33]

Just as he reached for her and blackness overtook her, BAM! Someone kicked in the door.

There, framed against the shining afternoon sun, stood the fat man Faith and Ryan had encountered before.

"Begone, you!" he said casually, smoking his cigar.

Health-and-Wealth hissed, recoiling as the sun burst through the doorway.

"I said leave, already," the fat man added, shooing the demon away with his hand.

As the sun pierced the void, Health-and-Wealth vanished as quickly as he'd appeared in all his demony evilness.

"Sun! They hate light. Just like in all the old stories," the fat man said happily. "Sorry—I'd pick you up, but I'm quite fat." He laughed.

Faith regained her strength and stood.

"Fairy tales! Always remember what you learned in the old fairy tales. Light kills the darkness, the demons, the danger. They're truer than you know," the fat man continued cheerfully.

"Ryan!" Faith said suddenly, remembering herself.

---

[33] This isn't the scene where she dies. That comes later. Uh . . . I mean . . . or does it?! MYSTERY! SUSPENSE! NARRATIVE TENSION! Man, I'm good at this.

"Yes, go get your companion. I'm sure he'll be fine. Only you must hurry—demons have a way of coming back again and again. And this time, he'll really be cross."

"Are you going to appear to save us every time we're in trouble?" she asked.

He laughed again. "No. That would be bad storytelling. I'm pushing it as it is." With a twinkle of his eye, he whirled away and left. "Now where did the wind take my hat!?" he shouted as he walked back up the road as fast as his tubby legs would take him.

Faith found Ryan sweating in the bed. His fever had broken, and his wound was miraculously healed.

"Ryan! We have to go!" she said.

"What?!" he said groggily, sitting up. "Why?"

"Health-and-Wealth is a demon, and the fat man saved us. It's a whole thing," she said.

"Wow. Well, can we at least stay the night?"

Faith rolled her eyes. "Have you learned nothing? I'd rather sleep on the Road than spend another second here."

Ryan sighed. "But the bed is so comfy."

She grabbed him by the arm and pulled him up. "Huh."

"What?"

"It's just weird. Health-and-Wealth was a demon. Yet, he healed you."

"Maybe it was really a curse and I'll turn into a lizard person before too long," Ryan said.

"No, I don't think so," she said, furrowing her brow and examining his leg. "I think . . . I think maybe his healing is real. But he uses it, and his powers, to grant wishes to get people to leave the Road. They're healed, but then they no longer feel the need to get to the King."

"You're smart," Ryan said, his mind still wrapped in a groggy fog. "I love you."

Faith rolled her eyes. "Come on. No falling in love with your guide. That's one of the rules. Let's get a move on."

CHAPTER 9:

EVANGELION

It's the job that's never started as takes longest to finish.

—Samwise Gamgee, *The Fellowship of the Ring*

I don't know why you're clapping. I'm talking about you!

—Paul Washer

They journeyed on for two and a half days. Hundreds of pages could be written on the beautiful sights they saw, their deep and meaningful conversations, and their slow but steady character growth.

But that would be so very boring for you. If you wanted endless descriptions of landscapes and traveling montages, you'd be reading a Robert Jordan novel. So, to speed things up here, I'm going to hit the fast-forward button and take you to the moment they entered the City of Evangelion.

The city was sprawling, one of the largest in the Dying Lands. Its wall encircled several square miles, packed with tens of thousands of followers of the King preparing for their journey to the Golden City. The most unique thing about Evangelion, and the first thing Ryan noticed as they drew near, was the large dome covering the entire city. It appeared to be made of glass or crystal and rose several hundred feet in the air at its highest point above the city center.

The domed city gleamed in the morning sun as they approached its western gate. The road here was paved and better cared for than it was in the wilds through which they'd come. Rough dirt and overgrown cobblestone turned into fine, freshly cut paved stones under their feet as they drew near.

Two guards stood blocking their path, each of them clad in shining silver armor and holding a gold-tipped spear.

"Hullo!" one shouted, holding his hand up. "State your business!"

"We're pilgrims," Faith replied before Ryan could answer. "We seek the Golden City, as do all pilgrims of the King."

"Really? Prove it," the guard answered, folding his arms. "These are dark times, and the integrity of the city must be preserved."

Faith threw up her arms. "We really don't have time for this."

"Here," said Ryan, rummaging around in his bag. "Here's the Book we got back there in the City of Destruction."

"Hrm." The guard took the Book and looked it over suspiciously. "You know, even the imposters have the Book."

"Here, then," said Ryan, pulling up his pant leg. "Here's the injury I sustained fighting that crazy demon bull thing. Err—it *was* there before. Some guy healed it." He gestured toward some scratches on his arms and neck. "Anyway, these were from Depression Bog or whatever it's called. So, yeah—we're pretty obviously pilgrims passing through."

"That's all very good. But I was thinking more like a set of questions," said the guard.

"What? How is some kind of pop quiz going to prove that we're going to the City?" asked Faith. Her cheeks were turning redder than her hair. "We're clearly pilgrims. Ryan—my friend here—his hair is still singed from the City of Destruction, for goodness' sake!"

"Sorry—I've got to be cautious. I'm going to quiz you. Answer all three questions right, and you'll be granted access to Evangelion."

"This is ridiculous," Faith muttered. "But fine. Go ahead. We're ready."

"Alright. First question: What small marsupial animal is referenced on page fifty-seven of the Book?"

"What's a marsupial animal?" asked Faith.

"I think it's like a ferret," said Ryan.

"Ferret . . . is correct!" answered the guard happily. "'*And the true pilgrim will be as shrewd as a demon bull and nimble as a ferret,*' is verse 117 of Chapter Four of the Book, as all real pilgrims know. Maybe you're true followers of the King after all!"

Ryan shrugged at Faith.

"Next question: how many miles long is the King's Road?"

Ryan shrugged at Faith again.

"That's not even in the Book anywhere!" Faith protested.

The guard smiled. "Ah, yes, but it *is* in the commentaries on the Book. We study the Book relentlessly here in Evangelion. There are entire volumes on the Road: its length, its width, date of construction, types of soils and gravels used. Famous pilgrims and travelers. All the relevant details. Any *true* follower would know these kinds of facts."

"Isn't it more important to, you know, actually walk the Road than to just study a bunch of useless facts about it?" asked Faith.

"That's a false dichotomy," replied the guard. "You can both study the Road *and* walk the Road. It's a fallacy to say that just because someone knows lots of interesting trivia about the Road, they're not actually walking it."

"Have you ever made for the Golden City then?" asked Ryan.

"What?"

"Well, you're saying you can both study the Road and walk it. So have you walked it?"

"That's beside the point!" said the guard. Now he was the one getting red in the face.

"All of that study, and I bet you *still* don't even know how long it is," said Ryan.

"Of course I do! It's 761 miles long exactly!"

Ryan smiled. Faith smiled. The guard's eyes went wide. "Oh, bother. I always do that."

"Our answer is 761 miles," said Ryan, crossing his arms in satisfaction.

"Fine, fine," grumbled the guard. "Third and final question: how many pilgrims have perished on the road so far?"

"Ten thousand, six hundred and seventy-two," said Faith immediately. "Now that one, I know. I've . . . I've seen too many of them die along the way to forget that."

The guard straightened up. "Well, I suppose you're probably not spies or Hollow Ones. You may enter. Stay as long as you like. We have the finest study materials for any pilgrim looking to make for the Golden City. May the King bless your stay here."

Ryan and Faith entered the city. Sprawling out before them was a meticulously arranged gridwork of houses and buildings. Townspeople scurried about like ants bustling from one building to another. Many carried large, leather tomes, or had eclectic collections of rolled-up scrolls tucked under their arms. They passed several bookshops as they walked toward the center of town. Colorful tents and awnings stretched across the streets, casting the road in bright oranges and purples.

The sun passed through the city's magnificent dome of glass, causing rainbow-colored fractals to dance around them. The effect was stunning. It was as though they were standing in a giant kaleidoscope streaked with every color of the rainbow and some that Ryan couldn't quite remember having existed in his own world. He was starting to see why it would be much more attractive to stay here than to venture into whatever lurked in the murky forest beyond.

Far in the distance, the eastern wall of the city loomed above them. Two large iron doors were shut fast against the horrors of the outside world. The effect was jarring: a city of color and light standing against a black sea of the unknown just on the other side.

Ryan's attention was brought back to his immediate surroundings as they arrived in the center of town. A magnificent stone building stood in front of them. It reminded Ryan of something . . . catheters? No, that wasn't the right word. *Cathedrals*! That was it. The building was reminiscent of cathedrals in his own world, though his world seemed like a rapidly fading dream unless he concentrated very hard on trying to remember it.

"Is . . . is this a church of some sort?" Ryan asked as he gawked up at the building, which must have been two or three hundred feet high. He didn't remember any of the cathedrals in his world being that tall.

"No. It's a school," Faith answered. She shielded her eyes from the sun with her hand as she joined Ryan's upward gaze. For once, she looked as awestruck as he did at the wonders of her own world. "You're looking at the King's University. Pilgrims come from all over to learn about the King, the Road, the journey—everything."

"No wonder that guy up there was so excited about a pop quiz," Ryan muttered.

The two walked up to the entrance. Two large iron doors stood shut. On them were carved thousands of names.

"Who are these people?" Ryan asked, squinting at the tiny print.

"The pilgrims. All the ones who have died so far."

"Oh." Ryan got to the end of the list on the right-hand door. He shuddered a bit as he realized there was still plenty of room for more.

Then—BANG! The door flew outward and smashed into his head with a deep thud.

"Ow," he said, stumbling backward.

A small man popped out. He stood no more than five feet high. He wore a monk's haircut and brown robes. He carried a large tome under his arm. A deep scar ran across the length of his forehead.

"I'm Mr. Theology!" he said happily. "You must be Faith and Ryan."

"How'd you know?"

"I know almost everything!" the man said, smiling a yellow, toothy grin. He may have read lots of books, but he clearly did not own a toothbrush. "I read about your coming in one of my books! *Prophecies and Foretellings of the Fourth Age of the Dying Lands, Volume III*, I believe it was. A ripper of a tale, that one is! Many people believe it to be a forgery, written several centuries after the Apostle Wendell was alive, but I don't buy it."

"Sorry to interrupt, but we are in a bit of a rush. And we need food and shelter," Faith said. "Just for the night, of course. Anything in your books about that?"

"Yes, in fact!" the funny little man replied. "We have rooms for you here at the University. One for each of you. Follow me!"

They followed Mr. Theology into the Cathedral of Learning, and what they saw took their breath away: a mountain range of books as far as the eye could see. While the city outside was arranged in meticulous detail, the books before them appeared to have no real rhyme or reason to their organization. Teetering towers of books of all shapes, sizes, and colors climbed out of sight into the spire above. Rainbow-colored sunbeams burst through the stained-glass windows of the hall. Somewhere, a tower of books toppled and fell, sending the sound of a crash echoing through the building.

It may not have been a church, but it was clearly hallowed ground for the citizens of Evangelion.

Mr. Theology led them through the winding maze of books, scrolls, and parchments, knowing just where to turn, as though he'd led hundreds and hundreds of doomed pilgrims through this labyrinth of literature before.[34] Left, left, right, left, straight, now leading them through a spiral of books until they began to ascend a spiral stone staircase. It wound up and up to dizzying heights and gave Ryan the faint memory of looking down at towering skyscrapers whenever he'd take a trip on the flying machines in his world. At last, they arrived at a hallway lit by blue glowing lanterns, and Mr. Theology guided them to a low wooden door. Stooping to enter, the trio saw a warm bed and a wooden table with fresh food laid out before them.

"This will be your room for the duration of your stay," said Mr. Theology.

"Well, we're just staying one day," Ryan answered.

"Yes, yes. Just one day," Mr. Theology said. "Of course, of course. Now, before you rest: by law, every citizen of Evangelion must be armed with a sword." He gestured toward a guard out in the hall. The guard brought a large wooden tray laden with several steel short-swords. "Select one—it will be your trusted companion as you travel on the King's Road."

The swords came in a variety of shapes and sizes, but one caught Ryan's eye: its hilt was inlaid with gold, and an emerald stone was set in its crossguard. A swooping, intricate design of diamond and silver ran along its sharpened edge.

"That one! I got dibs on that one!" Ryan said, grabbing for it.

Faith rolled her eyes. After thinking for a moment, she selected a more humble offering: a sturdy steel shortsword without pomp or

---

[34] Of course, as you know, he had. All of them had died, most of them in horrible ways. Peter Burnsides, just a few months before, had tried to make the journey. He'd made it all the way through Evangelion. I personally was rooting for him. But, alas, the Nameless One of the Tunnels of the Yawning Dark has to feed sometime, and poor Peter was unlucky enough to step out of Evangelion just before his breakfast time. Don't worry, though—Faith and Ryan will be safe. Well, at least from the Nameless One of the Tunnels of the Yawning Dark.

flash. It looked dull and well-worn, as though it had seen its share of use over the years. "This will do," she said.

Mr. Theology led Faith to her room so the weary pilgrims could rest.

Each of them had a window looking out over the city of Evangelion. Ryan's window faced east. The view was breathtaking. A large, rugged mountain jutted out of the landscape, towering above the rest of the range that lined the eastern horizon, cast red in the rays of the late evening sun. Though at times it disappeared around bends and under creeping trees, Ryan could just make out the King's Road snaking its way toward the peak and up and over the very top. He sighed. They still had a long way to go.

Ryan and Faith both slept for well over fourteen hours, waking up in the mid-late morning. While waking up early to get a jumpstart on the day is a good thing, as everyone knows, once in a while, humans just need to sleep for fourteen hours with no judgment. Eventually, Ryan joined Faith in the common room at the end of the hall, and they shared a delicious breakfast of eggs, bacon, toast, and potatoes. If I had the opportunity to eat human food, I think I'd make a beeline for the cheese, but close behind that would be the bacon. It smelled delicious.

"You look nice," Faith said, laughing.

"What?" Ryan said with a mouthful of fried potatoes.

She laughed again. "You didn't use the mirror in your washroom, did you?"

Ryan reached up and felt his face and the top of his head. His hair stuck straight up, and he was pretty sure there was drool dried to his chin. He shrugged. "Sometimes you just need to sleep for fourteen hours."

See? I told you.

Mr. Theology then joined them in the common room and offered to give them a guided tour of the University. He showed them floors and floors of classrooms, common areas, dormitories—room after room filled with pilgrims studying the King and the way to the Golden City. Classrooms were filled with the sounds of lively debates about the exact nature of the Golden City, minutia about the prophecies of the pilgrims, trivia concerning the Hollow Ones, and on and on. Rarely did these students of the University venture outside the walls of the building itself, and never did they leave Evangelion at all.

At length, Mr. Theology suggested they take some time to explore the city: "You'll learn much here and meet lifelong friends. Take your time, and enjoy your stay."

"Maybe we should stay a little longer after all," said Ryan as the two walked through the market. "Just one more day."

A week went by. Then two. Then three. Every day, they purposed to leave the following morning, but every day, the beautiful rain-bowed sunrise, the warmth and comfort of the dome, the stacks and stacks of books and entertainment and learning, all beckoned them to stay, whispered to them to delay the journey just one more day. Eventually, something strange started to happen: the more they learned in Evangelion, the more they forgot. They forgot about the imminent danger, the destruction of the land, the Hollowplague, the ringing of the bell, and the Golden City itself. Of course, they knew the Golden City existed. But it became a kind of head knowledge: a subject you study in school from a distance, not a real place you could get to by journeying on the King's Road.

The longer they stayed, the more comfortable they got. They explored the length and breadth of the city, always finding some new group of pilgrims to glean information from. Mr. Theology proved a constant source of knowledge and trivia about the Dying Lands, the Road, the Golden City, and the King Himself. He outfitted them with new clothing and outer cloaks, sturdy leather covers for their copies of the Book, and everything else they'd need for their journey.

But strangely, despite the stacks and stacks of books in the University, Faith and Ryan never once found a copy of the King's Book in all the University. Mr. Theology claimed he had many translations of it, but they never did see one.

A few days later, while exploring the city, they happened upon a group of pilgrims who called themselves the Evangelion Association for Political Engagement. The EAPE was meeting in the town square just outside the University, gathering for a political meeting and protest.

"What do you do here in Evangelion?" Ryan asked the group's leader, who introduced himself as Mr. Political Engagement.

"We petition the powers and rulers of this world—kings, lords, nobles, that sort of folk—and ask them to pass laws that are more favorable to pilgrims," replied Mr. Political Engagement.

"But why?" Ryan asked. "I thought we were just supposed to be passing through the Dying Lands?"

"Well, of course," he said. "Of course we are. But we still want to live lives of comfort while we're here. And Evangelion, despite being full of pilgrims, has become a respected institution here in the Dying Lands. We have to maintain that level of respect and engagement with the world."

Ryan opened his mouth to protest, but it seemed to make a kind of sense to him now.

The meeting went on for several hours, with the EAPE debating some new law that restricted pilgrims from moving along certain sections of the Road or put restrictions on how they were to walk and how they were to dress and what kinds of things they were allowed to say. It was the position of the EAPE that they could come to some kind of compromise with the local lord who enacted these laws.

Ryan and Faith found this all very boring, as did I. Mr. Political Engagement, once you got him going, could talk for *hours*. I'll cut all that out and just tell you the next important thing that happened. Let's check in with Ryan and Faith later that afternoon.

After eating a fine lunch at one of Evangelion's world-famous potlucks, Ryan and Faith emerged onto the streets of the city to see a hilarious sight: a group of pilgrims all hopping on one foot through the alleyway.

"Greetings!" their leader called out breathlessly as he hopped along like a flamingo on crack. "I'm Mr. Legalist!"

"We're Ryan and Faith," Faith responded. "What on earth are you doing?"

"Why, we're hopping!" Mr. Legalist said. "The better question is why aren't you hopping with us?"

"Why would we hop?"

"Well, it's the rule!" Mr. Legalist replied.

"It's not in the Book anywhere," Faith said. "Well, at least, I don't think so."

"Quite right you are," Mr. Legalist said. "We made the rule up. But it's a good one. You see, by hopping, you put less wear on your other foot! Our rule is you only can go down the road if you hop exactly four hours and then alternate feet, all day long. Anyone who doesn't do this isn't qualified to go down the King's Road."

"Why would you follow a rule that makes things so difficult on yourselves?" asked Faith as the group hopped by.

"To weed out fake pilgrims, of course!" Mr. Legalist called back as he passed by. "You really ought to try it sometime! Come to one of our meetings at the Evangelion Legalist Society. Just don't be late! Every Thursday at 9:00 a.m. sharp!" They hopped along and out of sight.

The next morning, Faith and Ryan were walking alongside the far eastern portion of Evangelion, near the gate that opened into the Blackmuck Forest. This part of the city was less populated, with many of the buildings standing empty. Though they had explored much of the city over the many weeks they had been there, they hadn't approached the gate, though they weren't sure why.

"Pilgrims! It's time to take action for the King!" shouted a voice. They saw a street preacher—not an uncommon sight in Evangelion—giving a sermon. He had few listeners. Those who passed through this part of the town in the shadow of the great wall and the iron gate didn't tend to tarry. "Wake up out of your stupor! Do not live your lives here in Evangelion! Pass on through to the Golden City!"

Something about his voice gripped Ryan and Faith. They stood rooted to the spot for nearly an hour as the man gave an impassioned plea for pilgrims to *do something* with their lives rather than rotting away in Evangelion.

"I beg you," he concluded. "Please—please. Don't die here. Press on toward the goal. Live and die for your King!" They had never heard someone so sincere. He stepped down and sat against the wall. One man clapped. Another man jeered. Most ignored him.

Ryan and Faith approached. "Hello," Faith said. "That was . . . well, it was something. You don't speak as these other preachers do. You preach as though you really believe it. As though the Golden City were something to be believed in and pursued, not just studied in a stuffy room full of books."

The man looked up, locking eyes with her. There was hurt and weariness there.

"Thank you," he said, looking away. "The name is Pastor."

"Hi, Pastor. I'm Faith. And this is Ryan. We've been here a few weeks as we prepare for the journey."

Pastor looked sad. "No. No, you probably haven't."

"What?"

"Follow me, if you will. But only if you're ready. You can't unsee what I'm about to show you."

Ryan shot a glance at Faith. Since they'd arrived in Evangelion, they really hadn't encountered any kind of opposition, resistance, warnings, or negativity at all. It had been all pep talks and learning and positive thinking. This felt different.

Pastor led the way down winding alleyways and corridors, through back streets and byways, until they arrived at a simple wooden door set in the side of a nondescript stone building. Pastor pulled out an iron keyring and flipped through it until he got to the key he was looking for. He unlocked the door. "Last chance," he said.

Ryan and Faith looked at each other. "Let's take the red pill," Ryan said at last.

"What?"

"Let's just . . . let's see how deep the rabbit hole goes."

"Huh?"

"Let's just go down."

They followed Pastor down the darkened steps. Down, down, down it went, until they were in utter blackness. But the darkness soon gave way to an eerie green glow that illuminated the steps from somewhere beneath.

They had been descending nearly a half-hour when the stairs opened onto a tall stone platform in a wide cavern. Some magic or other force illuminated the yawning chamber with a dead and morbid green. The landing on which they stood towered some fifty feet above an uneven ground of dirt and rock. Majestic stone pillars rose to the ceiling of the chamber. As their eyes adjusted to the light, the pilgrims could make out small stone structures dotting the landscape all the way to the horizon. There were thousands and thousands of them stretching as far as their eyes could see.

"What is this? Some kind of underground city?" an awestruck Ryan asked.

"This isn't a city. It's a graveyard," Faith whispered, taking his hand.

She was right. The stone mounds were markers. Row after row of tombstones stabbed the putrid, musty air like rotten teeth.

Pilgrims, followers of the King, professors, scholars, students—all had met their end here in the domed safety of Evangelion. There was no dark magic at work here, no spell that made them stay and wither away and die. They had just never wanted to leave the comfort and safety of the city. They had never left the iron gates and continued on their journey, for staying was much more comfortable.

"This is just horrible," Ryan said. "How do we escape this fate?"

Pastor sighed. "Few do. They stay for a few days, then a few weeks, then . . . it's usually too late after that."

"Well, it's a good thing we've only been here a few days then."

"That's . . . that's what I need to tell you," Pastor replied. "Evangelion is a good place, don't get me wrong. But there's something sinister about it. Something draws you in and makes you never want to leave the safety and comfort of this . . . bubble."

He looked at them. "You have been here for three months."

"What?!" Ryan exclaimed. "There's . . . there's no way. We got here on a . . . a Tuesday, I think. And then . . . and then . . ." he held up his hands to count, but it was no use. They knew Pastor was right. They had wasted months here, doing nothing but dawdle as the Dying Lands slowly slunk toward destruction. The thought of what was happening in the outside world as they tarried horrified them.

"What do we do?" Faith whispered at length in the green gloom, slowly backing away from the horrid sight.

"Flee. Flee as though your lives depended on it. Because, well, they do. And take this." Pastor handed Ryan a tiny scroll. "Open this when you have great need—but only when it's your last possible choice. You'll know."[35]

"When will you follow?" asked Faith as they walked back up the steps into the light of Evangelion. Its rainbow-glossed beauty seemed to fade.

"We should stock up. Get some supplies before we go," Ryan said.

"No!" Pastor shouted. Then more calmly: "No. Just go. Too many pilgrims have heard my plea only to go back for a few things and never return. You have your swords. You have your Books. You have your scroll. And you have the favor of the King. That is all you need."

Pastor led them up the steps, through the winding streets back to the crooked, rusty iron doors. He pulled out an old-looking key and unlocked them. "No one has left this way for months, years even. Many say they want to take the Road, but few follow through. My prayers are with you. Now go. Perhaps, if the King wills it, I will catch up with you in a few weeks' time."

"Goodbye, Pastor. And thank you—we are forever in your debt."

He smiled sadly. "I'll see you in the Golden City. May the King bless your journey."

They slipped through, and the iron doors slammed shut behind them. The branches of the Blackmuck Woods reached for them like greedy arms.

---

[35] I know this seems like an overused trope, but hey. It's a dream. Kind of. I mean, it really happened. But it's also a dream/vision-type thing. Sometimes, it's OK for the hero to be given a token that is only to be used in his darkest hour. Hey, even J. R. R. Tolkien did it.

CHAPTER 10:

The Blackmuck Woods

A witch ought never to be frightened in the darkest forest, Granny Weatherwax had once told her, because she should be sure in her soul that the most terrifying thing in the forest was her.

—Terry Pratchett, *Wintersmith*

Ryan and Faith looked back toward Evangelion's exit. Unlike the entrance, which had been warmly lit, pristine, and welcoming, this place was overgrown with weeds and thick vines whose tendrils had almost completely concealed the crooked old door. A small lamp which hung over the door was rusted and without a light. It looked like no one had come that way for a very long time. That, of course, is because no one had.

"Faith, look," Ryan said, pointing up and through the glass dome of the city, toward the City of Destruction. Meteorites rained down like hail stones. The orange glow of the city burned closer now. As they had lollygagged in the safe, comfortable bubble of Evangelion, the world had been slipping slowly toward its destruction.

"What if we're too late? What if the lands are destroyed before we can make it to the Golden City to wake the King?"

Faith looked sadly at the burning of the only world she had ever known. She shifted her pack on her shoulders and turned to the woods. "All we can do is be faithful now. We can't change the past. We have to trust the King will use our efforts, as faltering as they may be."

The bright lights, cool air, and smiling faces were gone now. The music of Evangelion could no longer be heard. The air was thicker, staler, and colder here. Ryan slowly scanned the ground in front of him, his eyes following the faint trace of a straight road that led through the center of the woods. He took one last, longing look at the warm city behind him and then turned to face the dangers ahead, casting the comfort of Evangelion from his mind with great effort.

The woods. All the warnings from the inhabitants of Evangelion, all the fear of those who spoke of the dark woods beyond the gate, suddenly made sense now. The trees were grey and rotted. The darkness around them was thick, but it ebbed and flowed like a living creature, giving them brief glances at the dead husks all around them. This place was hollow. Ryan was starting to understand why it was so attractive for pilgrims to stay in Evangelion forever rather than risk the dangers of the Road.

The soupy blackness seemed to pull at the hairs on their arms, then at their skin, then at their limbs, then enveloping them with corpse-like arms, beckoning them deeper in the forest. Lining the path amid dead, rotting brush, were trees—at least that's what they appeared to be at first glance. Ryan narrowed his eyes and focused on the nearest tree, and then his eyes widened in horror.

"Is . . . is that a face?" he said.

The bark of the tree seemed twisted in one place, forming what appeared to be closed eyes, a nose, and a gaping mouth, frozen in a scream, or maybe a roar, or perhaps a laugh.

"They say these trees are what grow when travelers are lost to the Blackmuck," said Faith, looking warily at the cavern of claw-like limbs stretched out before them. "When travelers are consumed by the

Blackmuck, their minds merge with its own, and they grow into these trees, forever frozen and consumed with thoughts of consuming more and more. Terrifying to look at, but harmless, I think."

Faith was partially right about the trees. I had to do a bit of digging in the Archives to confirm her story. She was wrong, though, about the trees being harmless. They weren't. And the pilgrims would soon find that out for themselves. Ho ho! I bet you're interested in what happens next now!

As they cautiously trudged forward, their eyes adjusted to the darkness. Their noses, however, would never really adjust to the foul smell suffocating them from all around. They could almost see the odor wafting up from the forest floor and oozing out from the malice-filled trees.

"Yeesh. It smells like a funeral home out here." Ryan had a faint subconscious memory of being in a funeral home, but it was a bad memory, so he pushed it from his mind and focused on his immediate surroundings. "A funeral home is like a graveyard," Ryan explained to Faith's inquisitive look.

"So you don't have graveyards in your world?"

Ryan thought back. "Yes," he said finally. "We do. But the funeral home is where we, I guess, say goodbye. Say some nice words about the person." He shrugged. "It doesn't matter, anyway. It's just to make us feel better."

"We do the same," Faith said, tugging at her sleeve. Ryan saw the Hollowplague protruding from beneath it. "But, it's kind of strange. I think the words we say there have some real meaning. We say people kind of, go on, I guess. Maybe to the Golden City. The Book isn't too clear on specifics."

"I believed that stuff when I was a kid," Ryan said as they walked into the ever-increasing darkness. "I mean, we didn't call it the Golden City. We called it . . . Heaven, I think. But I outgrew that. Life kicked that belief out of me pretty quick."

"All children believe in the Golden City, of course," Faith said. "But that doesn't make it any less true. Sometimes I wonder if the children are smarter than we. They're purer, untouched by the troubles of the journey. Maybe it's foolish, but I just know, perhaps instinctively, that everyone moves on to another place after death."

They heard a low moan come from the woods to their right.

Faith pulled her cloak in closer. "Except the Hollow Ones. They just linger."

They traveled for several days along the road that wound through the inky blackness pressing in all around. The trees, ever so gradually and ever so slightly, moved in closer, choking out the King's Road. A craggy root here and there ran under the dirt path, causing them to stumble now and again. The light of the sun struggled to pierce the darkness above them, and the gloom grew greater by the hour. The gloom was thick, palpable—a swirling fog of blackness encircling them.

The woods were not entirely uninhabited, though. They came across several hordes of Hollow Ones wandering aimlessly through the trees, but thankfully, they were some ways off and did not notice them. They also saw several villages in various states of ruin and disrepair, but the townspeople eyed the travelers with suspicion and scurried indoors before they could say "hello." The farther they got from Evangelion, the more scarce these dwellings became, until Faith and Ryan truly felt they were alone out here in the great Blackmuck Woods.

Finally, one morning—at least, they were pretty sure it was morning—the path had become almost impossible to see, and they inched forward, feeling along with their feet, their hands outstretched lest they stumble again.

"What are we supposed to do now?" Ryan asked, despairing as he moved forward one feeble step at a time. Evangelion was looking better and better, graveyard or no.

"Just keep on the path. I'm not sure what else we can do at this point," said Faith as she opened her Book and began to flip through it, her eyes struggling to make out any of the words in the swaying, inky darkness.

Opening to a chapter entitled "The Woods," Faith found only a single phrase, surrounded by empty parchment.

Just stay on the path.

"What does it say?" asked Ryan.

"It's telling us to just stay on the path."

"That's it?"

"Yeah," replied Faith, squinting once more at the mostly blank page.

Great. Just great.

"Well, it sure would be nice if we could see the freakin' path," muttered Ryan to himself.

As the two fumbled forward one step at a time, they began to hear faint noises—clanking sounds—up ahead. As they got closer, they could hear the grinding sounds of metal on metal, and the clanking, whirring, and growling of what sounded almost like steam locomotives.

"Is that a train up ahead?" asked Ryan.

"I shall just assume a 'train' is something from your world, and you've forgotten that I haven't the faintest idea what anything in your world is like."

"Oh yeah. Sorry."

As they got closer, the undulating blackness began to clear—not because of any kind of light, though. As the darkness dissipated, Ryan and Faith were able to make out the source of the clanking, whirring, and growling. Up ahead, on both sides of the path, were gleaming metal platforms, each holding what looked like spinning bronze fan blades, creaking, groaning, and clanking, blowing the dark fog off the path.

There was a small clearing. The "trees" surrounding the path had been chopped down and were lying in a pile of split logs off to the side. And now, Ryan and Faith could see the path branched off in two different directions.

From up ahead, someone was approaching.

CHAPTER 11:

THE TOOLS IN THE TOWER

Progress means getting nearer to the place you want to be. And if you have taken a wrong turn, then to go forward does not get you any nearer. If you are on the wrong road, progress means doing an about-turn and walking back to the right road; and in that case the man who turns back soonest is the most progressive man.

—C. S. Lewis, *The Case for Christianity*

Get woke, go broke.

—John Ringo

"Well, aren't you two a cute couple!"

Faith grabbed Ryan by the arm and cautiously drew her sword.

Ryan looked past the rattling fans in the direction of the voice but couldn't see anything. He suddenly wished he, too, had a sword. *Oh yeah,* he remembered as his hands found the hilt of the glittering weapon at his side. He'd had it hanging off his belt for months and months. Yet he'd never had to use it in the safety of Evangelion. His body tensed, preparing for something. He didn't know what. The only real fighting experience he had in his other world came from video games and one altercation with a bully when he was in the third grade. He had been knocked out for twelve seconds then, but that's an epic story for another day. If I'm ever commissioned to transcribe that dream for you, it will have to be a trilogy.

Something about Faith grabbing Ryan's arm made him stand tall and ready for action.

Out from behind a tree stepped a tall blonde woman with a wide smile. Ryan relaxed a little.

"Don't worry, hon. I'm no danger to ya! I just heard you two making your way down our path and wanted to be sure to welcome you to our fine neck o' the woods! What are your names?"

"Well, we're not really a couple," Ryan replied. "We're just travelers. My name's Ryan. This is Faith."

Ryan thought he saw the woman's smile disappear slightly when she heard their names, but only for a second. She quickly recovered and smiled warmly at them both. "I am so sorry! I should introduce myself. I am Mrs. Deconstruction, but you can just call me Mrs. D. I live in that lovely little clearing over yonder with my partner, Mr. System. We help pilgrims just like you find what they're looking for. Have you read my book? It's a bestseller in the Dying Lands!"

Ryan and Faith studied the tall blonde woman for a moment. She was very well dressed—not in the garish style of the Smiling Preacher, but one could tell her clothing was expensive and that she gave great attention to her appearance. Her face was sharp, beautiful, and proud.

She smiled at them, waiting for an answer.

"Well? Have you? If not, you should! It's called *Forget Everything You Know and Listen to Me Because I'm the First Person to Really Figure Things Out*. I wrote it just for pilgrims like you!"

"Um, that's the title?" asked Ryan. "'*Forget Everything You Know and Listen to Me Because I'm the First Person to Really Figure Things Out*'? How'd you manage to fit all that on the cover?"

Faith elbowed him.

Mrs. Deconstruction smiled curtly but ignored Ryan's quip.

"You see, that book you have there," she motioned to the leather-bound Book Ryan was holding. "It ain't easy to understand all the time, is it?"

Ryan and Faith looked at each other. "No," Ryan replied. "Not always, I guess."

"Exactly! You see, that book was written ages ago by many ignorant, uneducated people who hadn't figured everything out the way I have. It has led many people astray who didn't take the time to understand and read it properly. That's why Mr. System and I put together our, well, our system! Follow me and I'll show you what I'm talking about."

She led them down an unmarked path until they were standing in a large clearing surrounded by trees on all sides. Ryan suddenly realized he hadn't paid attention to which branching path they had taken. Mrs. Deconstruction looked back, and as if she were reading his mind, said, "Oh, don't worry, hon. You're still on the road. That's why we're here. To make sure you stay that way!"

The noises were deafening now, like the sound of fifty steam locomotives running at once. Large metal blades attached to belts, chains, pulleys, and shuddering steam engines surrounding the clearing kept the darkness of the forest at bay. In the center of the clearing stood a colossal metal tower made of what appeared to be copper, brass, or bronze. It was bristling with gadgets, gauges, spinning gears, and flickering lights. At the foot of the tower, several massive steam generators roared, powering all the whining machines and groaning gadgets.

Faith stood and gawked at the monstrosities.

Ryan looked at her with amusement and chuckled to himself. "I guess you're not familiar with steampunk."

"What's a steampunk?" Faith tilted her head and looked at him curiously.

Ryan drew a blank. He couldn't remember.

"Um, I dunno. The word just came to me. Maybe I dreamed it once."

At the base of the tower, a release valve hissed loudly, and a bronze door haphazardly adorned with a clutter of gears, pipes, and pulleys opened with a creak and a groan. In the doorway stood a short, round man with wild black hair and a handlebar mustache. Concealing his eyes were thick goggles covered with devices, extra lenses, and magnifiers.

"Hey hoo hoo! Welcome to the Ivory Tower!" he called out in a high-pitched, jittery voice.

He beckoned them with his hand to cross the clearing and come in the front door. Mrs. Deconstruction smiled at them reassuringly.

"Come on in with me! That's my life partner, Mr. System.[36] He shall provide you with everything you need for your journey."

Faith looked at Ryan, her brow tightening.

"Maybe we should be going," she said.

"Nonsense!" said Mr. System. "You need to rest from your journey. Let me show you my inventions and equip you with some tools!"

"You can't tell since we're surrounded by the woods, but it's nearly midnight," said Mrs. Deconstruction. "Why don't you rest for the night, and we'll get started in the morning!"

Faith looked uneasy, but the mention of the hour made her yawn. Ryan was feeling exhausted as well.

Mrs. Deconstruction led them to a rusty metal room with several iron bunk beds lined up against the walls. Edison bulbs hanging from a jumbled mess of pipes, gauges, and gears sent eerie, scattered shadows dancing across the walls.

---

[36] Mr. System is from your world, strangely enough. He's a university law professor in Seattle who dabbles in comic book art, and he's currently sleeping soundly after drinking a little too much last night.

"I know it looks a little cold, but it's the best we can muster in these hostile woods. I assure you the beds are comfortable. You'll need all the brainpower you can muster tomorrow. We have so much to show you!"

Ryan and Faith were so exhausted at that point, they could muster no objections. They crawled into their metal beds and fell asleep to the sound of roaring generators.

The sound is actually kind of soothing, thought Ryan. And he drifted off to sleep.

While they slept, both Ryan and Faith were whisked off to other universes. Faith landed in Universe #XA-31C, a world that had experienced heat death eons ago. She met a race of Boltzmann brains floating through the galaxy and spent a lifetime with them.

Ryan's mind was dropped into #XU-43B. Remember that one? The one I mentioned in the introduction, inhabited by seventeen-dimensional beings with razor sharp claws and flesh-ripping pincers? Yeah—that one. He battled the multidimensional monsters to help save an enslaved race of peaceful fish-creatures, and lost. He lost badly. Gruesomely. But that's a story for another time.

After a fitful sleep, Ryan awakened with a start, clutching his abdomen where he was sure he had been disemboweled by an alien laser pincer. In an instant, he forgot the dream. The generators were off. All was silent. It was dark in the early morning hours. Mr. System and Mrs. Deconstruction were standing over them, peering down with dark, hawklike eyes.

"Come with us," they said in unison.

OK, this is creepy, thought Ryan.

Faith sat up groggily and stretched, her red hair a mess. "Where are we going?"

"You'll see! We're so excited to get you set up and fully equipped to follow the path!" said Mr. System in his cheery yet shrill voice.

Mr. System led them to a large room filled with stacks of books and strange mechanical devices. "This is where you'll find everything you need to properly understand and live out the Book," he said. "Please sit."

Ryan and Faith sat down at two little wooden desks like kids in elementary school.

"Besides Mrs. D's amazing book, *Forget Everything You Know and Listen to Me Because I'm the First Person to Really Figure Things Out*,[37] which you absolutely must read, you will need three things." Mr. System reached into a metal box and removed several items. The first looked like a pair of goggles made of thick glass and a leather strap, which he firmly attached to Ryan's head. The second was a golden pair of shears, which he put in Ryan's hand. The third was a whip.

"This is your lens, your analytical tool, and your implicit bias remover. You will need all three of these to understand the Book properly."

"This is it? Can't we get a laser gun or some cool power armor[38] or something?" said Ryan.

"Ha ha. Very funny, lad," said System, twirling his mustache. "Put on the goggles."

Ryan fit the leather strap around his head. He was disoriented by the thick glass lenses in the goggles.

---

[37] Through a strange sequence of dreams, a parallel version of this book became a bestseller in Universe #88-V3Y, where all the underwater inhabitants of the planet Rucktoid organized their entire society around it for over ten thousand years. Things were going pretty well until another author came along with the bestseller *You've Been Deceived This Whole Time And I Alone Have The Answer,* which led to a civil war that lasted five centuries and led to the extinction of every life form on the planet. It was one of the first tales I ever recorded for the Archives. On the bright side, Rucktoidian music is simply sublime. Or was. Sad.

[38] Ryan played way too many video games, but even I must admit, a laser gun and power armor would have helped them out quite a bit on this particular journey.

He looked at the book in his hand and couldn't believe what he saw. Squinting through the goggles, he saw the lines and dots in the ancient runes of the book shifting and morphing into different words.

Faith put the goggles on, looked at Ryan once, let out a small shriek, and then ripped them off with disgust.

"If you read the book with these glasses on," explained Mr. System, "you will see mostly what you're supposed to see. But the magic of the goggles isn't strong enough for every passage in the book. For some of the more stubborn pages, you will need this golden analytical tool."

Ryan turned it around in his hand and looked at Mr. System skeptically.

"But this is literally just a giant pair of scissors."

Mr. System winced. "Seriously? Please. Don't use such crude language here. These aren't 'scissors.' They are analytical tools to help keep you on the right path."

Faith looked on suspiciously, arms crossed. "And what's the whip for?"

"Ugh! Again with the crude language! This is an implicit bias remover. People sometimes react to the lenses and analytical tools. This bias remover helps to remind you of your shortcomings and motivate you to use these essential tools at all times. You should use it on yourself often."

Faith had heard enough. "Welp, I think we should be going!" she said as she abruptly pushed out her chair and got up.

"So soon?" said Mrs. Deconstruction. "But I haven't even given you copies of my book yet! Did I mention it's a bestseller?"

"Yeah, I think it's time to go." Faith was speed-walking toward the door. "Ryan, you coming?"

Still wearing the goggles, Ryan turned and looked at Faith. He was horrified by what he saw. The magic of the lenses had changed her form, her face. Her face was misshapen, her back hunched. The goggles had turned Faith into a hideous creature. No wonder she had jumped and ripped her own goggles off when she saw Ryan.

"You won't get far without your tools!" Mr. System called after them. "Our followers live in the woods, and they won't like it when they see you without your tooools!"

Ryan ripped his goggles off and bolted for the front door after Faith. They shot out of the tower and into the clearing.

But they were not alone.

Emerging from the dark woods into the clearing were hundreds of travelers. They were all wearing those strange goggles. In their right hands they held razor-sharp golden shears. In their left, they all held whips. Methodically, mechanically they began whipping themselves. Each was crying something different—"I'm unworthy!" "I'm sorry!" "I'll do better!"—as tears streamed down their faces. Some pulled out their Books and cut out pages, screaming in anger at things they did not like within. As one, in unison, they locked eyes with Ryan.

The one in front, a scrawny white man with a thin, scraggly red beard, smiled at him and held out a whip. "Your turn. Join us."

The rest of the crowd quieted down as they listened for Ryan's response.

"Faith, hold on to me," he said, not taking his eyes off the mob, which slowly closed in on them, step after droning step. "Go slow. No sudden movements."

"JOIN US!" the one with the red beard said again, irritation in his voice. "Do you think you're better than us? Following a book written by unenlightened sinners, without any of Mr. System's tools to guide you? HAVE SOME HUMILITY! ADOPT THE SYSTEM!" He spat the words, as well as his spit, in Ryan's face.

"Deconstruct, have some humility, adopt the system," the crowd echoed dutifully, excitedly, fidgeting like antsy children before recess. They seemed to creep and lurch in closer and closer with every passing moment.

More zombie-like travelers, all equipped with their "tools," emerged from the woods, their eyes fixed on Ryan and Faith. They all twitched with anticipation as they echoed the mantra "deconstruct, have some humility, adopt the system."

They chanted as they swayed back and forth slowly, but as they approached Ryan and Faith, they began to twitch, as if they were pit bulls being held back by their master's chain.

Mrs. Deconstruction called out to them from her tower. "Do you realize how many people have been enslaved and abused by the words in that book?" she said. "Don't you understand that without our special way and our special tools, you are destined to become the hideous, deformed creatures you appear to be?"

Ryan looked back. Mrs. Deconstruction was looking at them through her own pair of goggles.

The scrawny man with the red beard looked at them expectantly. "So what will it be?" he said. The zombies that now filled the clearing twitched with nervous energy, as though ready to pounce.

Ryan's mind raced. He and Faith scanned the clearing for some avenue of escape, but saw none. He realized they would have to make a beeline for the woods. In the thick, soupy darkness, they might not ever find the path again, but at that point, they had to try.

"So what will it be? Will you take the tools?" said Redbeard again. "ADOPT THE SYSTEM!"

Ryan squared his shoulders and managed to squeak out an answer. He didn't sound very sure of himself.

"Um . . . no?"

"CANCEL THEM!" screamed Redbeard, spit flying from his mouth. The zombie army brandished their whips and razor-sharp scissors, which were no longer merely tools for deconstructing the Book and punishing themselves. They were weapons for eliminating outsiders.

Ryan and Faith locked eyes. *Run.*

They made a beeline for the nearest wall of inky black woods as the mob gave chase. As they ran, they heard screams that sounded like a combination of rage and agony.

Almost there . . .

As they bounded closer to the woods, the green grass of the clearing gave way to black roots that jutted up from the ground like stalagmites in a cave.

Then the roots, with a series of loud cracks and groans, began to move. Black, twisted tendrils began to push up through the grass, writhing and reaching. Viney, moss-covered fingers grabbed and clawed, reaching for Ryan's ankles and arms. The trees, or whatever malevolent entity possessed them, would not let them escape.

Faith's left foot caught one of the roots and she tripped, landing hard on the ground.

"Christian!" she shouted.

Ryan—who was somewhat surprised that he responded to the name "Christian"—looked back and saw Faith on the ground as the mob descended on her like a swarm of insects. He gulped and ran back to her. They were on her now with scissors and whips brandished. He only had a few seconds.[39]

As he dove into the snarling crowd, he reached out for Faith's hand. A hundred sharpened shears snapped for her. One took a lock of her red hair. "ADOPT THE SYSTEM!" the screams continued.

He found Faith's hand. *Gotcha!*

Then, scrawny Redbeard drove a pair of scissors through Ryan's leg. A searing pain shot from his calf as the blades plunged through muscle, skipped off the bone, and sank into the ground. Redbeard looked at Ryan with a wicked grin of triumph.

---

[39] And, of course, he had completely forgotten about his sword. Humans are not a particularly bright species, and Ryan was not a particularly bright human. If I haven't mentioned that yet.

Ryan finally remembered his sword. He reached for it, simultaneously realizing he'd never used a sword before—at least, not that he could recall.

In reality, he had used a sword three times: once in universe XB-433-U against a blob-like creature who had attacked his little brother, once in universe AA-627 in a duel for a fair maiden's honor, and the third time in universe C-6H-2TU during a murderous rampage against a village of peaceful mechanical creatures. Well, that last time it was more of a laser stick-type weapon, but we'll count that as a sword.

None of that experience would help him here. He didn't remember any of it. I'm always amazed by how little information human brains can hold.

He gripped the elaborately bejeweled handle and pulled it from its scabbard. It was a beautiful weapon. Even with the chaos and the searing pain in his leg, he couldn't help but notice the way the sunlight glinted off the edge. The crowd of zombies, however, didn't seem to notice at all. They just kept coming, chanting and snarling and howling.

He closed his eyes and swung wildly, like a blindfolded kid trying to hit a piñata at a birthday party. So unimpressive. What does the Creator see in this guy, anyway? Whatever it is, He never told me. I couldn't find any clues in the Archives either.

The sword swung harmlessly through the air with a whistle, again and again. And then, finally, and very much by luck, it connected with Redbeard's neck.

Ryan opened one eye to see the carnage he had inflicted. But Redbeard was still there grinning his wicked grin. The beautiful sword had done nothing and was now shattered in sparkly pieces that littered the ground.

"Oh, come on!" Ryan shouted.

Two more zombies brandishing golden shears descended on Faith, as she frantically tried to crawl away. Ryan was pinned on his back, and his view of the sky was blotted out by a mass of writhing arms holding golden blades.

This is it, he thought as he closed his eyes and prepared for the death blow to come.

Wait!

Ryan's eyes snapped open as he remembered the scroll given to him by Pastor back in Evangelion, to be used "in the hour of his most desperate need."

Well, I think this qualifies, he thought as he reached for the scroll, pulled it out, and opened it.

No magical lightning or concussive blast emerged from the rolled-up paper to vanquish his enemies. No white light shot out to blind the assailants. Ryan wasn't unreasonable to have expected this—there are many magical scrolls in many realities that possess such power. When I was new to my position (only three thousand years in), I opened one of these scrolls in the Archives and made a huge mess. The other Narrators and Storykeepers haven't let me hear the end of it for eons.

This scroll was different. Ryan unrolled it and saw two words, written squarely in the middle of the parchment in red ink.

Walk forward.

Ryan cursed. *In my hour of desperate need, huh? THANKS A LOT!*

Ryan crumpled up the scroll and jammed it in his pocket. Only a sword would get them out of this jam, and Faith had a sword too. He only had moments to act. He grabbed the sword from Faith's belt, gripped it tightly, and thrusted—this time less wildly—and this time, with his eyes open.

Once again, the sword connected with Redbeard's shoulder and effortlessly lopped off his arm, which flopped onto the ground helplessly, still clutching the blade that was still in Ryan's leg.

The rest of the goggle-wearing zombies leapt back in a flurry of outraged shrieks and screams. The screams spread through the entire crowd as they all stared at Faith and Ryan through their goggles, their faces twisted in outrage. The screams grew louder, but none of them dared step forward. They were too afraid of the humble-looking sword Ryan now held in his hand.

Faith gave him a look.

"You gonna say 'I told you so'?" Ryan said defensively.

"Just help me up, Ryan."

Throughout the clearing, zombie disciples continued to stare. Through their goggles, Ryan could see their eyes bulging with unspeakable rage. Still, none of them moved. They began to sway back and forth once again, quietly chanting their slogan: "Adopt the system . . . adopt the system." Then, one by one, they grabbed onto each other's shoulders and walked as one back into the woods behind the Ivory Tower. Their chanting, punctuated by the occasional crack of an "implicit bias remover" across someone's back, disappeared into the Blackmuck Woods.

Ryan turned around to look at the wood on the opposite end of the clearing from where they had entered. The black tentacle roots of the trees had buried themselves back in the ground and the forest had gone silent. Reaching into his pocket, his fingers found the crumpled-up piece of paper. Ryan cursed again under his breath at the memory. Even so, the words of the scroll, "Walk forward," played through his head.

Through the dark fog and the trees, he could barely make out an overgrown brick path laid out before them.

Walk forward.

Ryan and Faith did just that.

CHAPTER 12:

THE SLIPPERY SLOPE

The safest road to hell is the gradual one, without signposts . . .

—C. S. Lewis, *The Screwtape Letters*

Life is pain, Highness. Anyone who says differently is selling something.

—The Man in Black, *The Princess Bride*

They limped into the dark woods once again, slowly putting one foot in front of the other. Ryan's leg throbbed with pain. When he looked down, he saw blood trickling out of the wound where the bearded man had stabbed him.

"That doesn't look good," Faith said. Ryan shot her a look. She laughed. "Sorry. I mean—it looks *fine*, and you'll be *just fine*."

He stuck his tongue out at her.[40]

The two sat down uneasily on the path in the middle of the woods, fully aware they were still surrounded by the frozen creatures who had tried to trip them up in the clearing. They were silent and unmoving, their faces still locked in grimaces and screams.

---

[40] Ryan didn't know it, but in Faith's world, sticking one's tongue out at a member of the opposite sex meant either "I love you" or "I would like to trade your father seventeen goats for your hand in marriage," depending on the dialect and contextual clues.

Faith pulled from her bag some cloth and a glass bottle filled with a swirling blue substance. She poured it on Ryan's wound, and instead of a sting, he felt a warm sensation. She began to gently wrap his leg in the bandage.

"You know, for all Evangelion's faults, I'm not sure we would have gotten by without their help," Ryan said, eyeing the now-empty potion bottle.

Faith nodded. "That's true." Ryan turned his attention to their immediate predicament, uneasily glancing from side to side at the frozen horrors all around.

"I'm sorry," he started. "I shouldn't have let us follow those two to the Ivory tower. We shouldn't have stayed."

He shuddered at the thought of Faith's monstrously deformed face that had appeared when he put on the goggles.

"When you looked at me through the goggles, what did you see?"

Faith paused the bandaging. She started to say something but fell silent.

"Was I a monster? Was I deformed?" Ryan pressed.

"No," said Faith. "It was sadder than that."

What's that supposed to mean?

"What did you see, Faith?"

Faith stood up slowly and looked down at Ryan squarely.

"Come on, get up. We'll talk about that later," said Faith, her hand extended.

Ryan decided to drop the subject.

They walked on in silence for a few hours. The woods remained silent. The glow from Faith's torch illuminated the path at their feet, keeping them from tripping. Slowly, the fog began to dissipate, and they stumbled out of the Blackmuck Woods into blinding sunlight.

"Huh," said Faith, turning to look back at the black woods they'd finally left behind.

"What is it?" Ryan asked.

"It's just, it felt like we were never getting out of there. Like we were in the very heart of it, nowhere near the end. And just like that, one step led us into the light."

Ryan started thinking about that, but his thoughts were interrupted by a sound somewhere up the road. It sounded like laughter.

"Woo-hoooooooo!" one voice cried up ahead. It sounded like an eight-year-old riding a roller coaster for the first time.

"Wheeeeeeeee!" called another.

Ryan and Faith's eyes adjusted to the bright light to see the path stretched out before them. It was no longer crumbling or in disrepair. Instead, pristine brick pavers formed a very narrow path. On each edge of the path were small guardrails with a logo reading "Chesterton's Railing Company" stamped into the metal. At the far end of the narrow way, many miles off, they could see a hill rising into the clouds, obscuring what looked like the light of a sunrise on the other side. Cutting sharply into the sky beyond the hill was a massive peak jutting up against the sun.

"Is the Golden City on the other side of those mountains?" Ryan asked.

"I don't know . . ." Faith said, squinting at the hill, the peak, and the light beyond.

Ryan could see why the railing had been installed, since on either side there were steeply sloped hills that were slick with a black, oily substance. The hills plummeted down hundreds of feet into a swirling black fog. It was impossible to see what was at the bottom. Yet everywhere, as far as the eye could see, people were sliding down the hills on either side of the path, giggling and cheering as they went.

"WHEEEEEEEEEE!" cried one pink-haired traveler on a sled as he slid down the hill at top speed and disappeared into the mist below.

"What is this place?" Ryan said to Faith.

"I'm not sure. Never made it this far before."

"This is weird. Pretty straightforward though, right? Just stay on the path and walk right down the middle."

Faith hesitated. "Well, it looks that way, but what is everyone else doing?"

Up ahead, a small group of travelers was gathered, preparing to walk around the bridge and make the journey toward the peak while carefully holding onto the slippery slope.

"Yooooo! What's up, guys? You traveling to the Golden City?"

A tan, sinewy man with shaggy blonde hair approached them and held out his hand in greeting. "My name's Good Times. I guide people across this great chasm. I got all the equipment you'll need—ropes, picks, climbing shoes, all the best gear to get you across safely!"

Ryan was confused. He peered beyond Good Times as the group of travelers ahead of him began to carefully inch their way along the oily slope.

"Um, why do we need a guide? There's a perfectly fine-looking stone path with a railing."

"Oh no—you don't wanna take that," said Good Times with a chuckle. He gestured toward the hills surrounding the valley. A row of towers sat like jagged teeth on the edge of the ravine, making the whole place look unsettlingly like a giant pair of jaws. "The Guardians of the Valley live in those towers.[41] They will shoot anyone who tries to take that path. Many travelers in the past tried to follow it. Never made it across. It's a deathtrap. That's why I'm here! To guide dudes like you!"

Ryan peered uneasily at the dark stone towers. An arrow slit was cut into each one. He could only see blackness within.

"But—what about the slippery slope?" Ryan asked.

[41] Little is known about the Guardians of the Valley. From their dark towers they shoot strange magical crossbows equipped with supersonic arrows that explode upon impact. The effect of their weapons is pretty gruesome. Legends say they are servants of the bald, bespectacled man who calls himself "The Devil," and they indiscriminately pick off travelers unless personally forbidden to do so by the King. That's all I could find about them in the Archives.

Good Times groaned. "WHAT? Are you kidding? You're gonna worry about a slippery slope? What's there to worry about? Just because there's a slippery slope doesn't mean you're gonna slip down it, man."

Another man walked up while Good Times was speaking. He had a balding head and patchy beard. On his nose was perched a pair of makeshift glasses that almost looked like they had been assembled using the pieces from goggles given out by Mr. System at the Ivory Tower. He strode up confidently and stood there smugly, his arms crossed and leg cocked to one side.

"Greetings," he said. "My name is Ackshully. You two look kind of worried about the wonderful open field up ahead. Adorable. You really can just relax, OK? Don't be so earnest. It's totally cringe."

Ryan paused. *If this guy only knew what our day has been like . . .*

"Aren't you worried about that massive slippery slope up ahead? Isn't it dangerous? Does anyone even know where it leads? Look how far off the path people are sliding . . ."

"Woah, woah, woah," said Ackshully. "Please. Slippery slope, really? How cliché. The slippery slope is a total fallacy, man."

Good Times piped in. "Yeah, bro, you have nothing to worry about. The field opened up before you is all about freedom! You can't limit yourself to the same old narrow views of how to get to the Golden City. There's a ton of valid ways to make it work and have a little more fun doing it! Besides, you can stay as close to the path as you want! You don't even need to slide down!"

"But there are people literally slipping down it right now."

Good Times and Ackshully whirled around just in time to see the group of travelers up ahead lose their footing and slide down the steep incline. They were laughing and giggling. Good Times shrugged. "Well, it looks like they're having fun to me!"

"Dude! Didn't you just say we wouldn't slip down the slippery slope? Look! What's up with that?"

"Well, if it's so dangerous, why does it look like everyone is having a blast?"

"But isn't the goal to get to the other side?"

"Of course, man! You'll be fine! I have all the equipment you'll need. You won't slide down the slippery slope. And even if you do, there are plenty of safe ways to get to the Golden City. Whatever you do, don't take the path in the middle, or you're dead."

A commotion in the woods behind them interrupted their conversation. Ryan turned around and his blood ran cold.

Out of the woods trudged nine goggle-wearing zombies from the Ivory Tower. They marched slowly. With their left hands they held onto the necks of the person in front of them. In their right hands, they carried their Bias Correctors, rhythmically cracking them across their backs as though engaged in some holy monastic ritual. They glanced at Ryan and Faith, but instead of rage, they looked at them with smugness. They began to chant, slow and sure:

"Thank You, King, that we are not like these other travelers! Thank You, King, that we are not like these other travelers!"

The horde trudged down the middle of the path in single file, keeping right in between the guardrails. Good Times grimaced, as though he knew what was about to happen. Ackshully still looked smug, and side-eyed Ryan and Faith as if to say, "Watch this."

The towers sprang to life. A distant *twang* rang out, and the zombie-person in the front of the line died quickly and horribly. Again, I really don't want to go into graphic detail of how his head exploded into a fountain of red gelatinous goo all over the path and the travelers behind him, so I'll spare you the horrific image. Shoot—maybe I shouldn't have written all that. Sorry. I'm not gonna bother erasing it now. I have a deadline with this thing and I'm kind of under the gun here. Where was I? Oh yeah—exploding heads.

Anyway, when the leader met his unfortunate demise, the eight behind him were seemingly snapped awake. They slowly took off their goggles and began to look around.

"So what do we do now?" one of them said, still shaking from the trauma.

"Well, we ain't moving forward, that's for sure." growled another. "We've been lied to. The Book led us astray."

They looked on either side of the path at the gently sloping cliffs going down in opposite directions. One of them turned back to Good Times and Ackshully, who had watched the whole episode with detached amusement. "Hey, you! Sinner! The one with the shaggy blonde hair! Is there a safer way to the Golden City?"

"Yeah, dudes—it's all safe. We've sent millions of travelers down these slopes with no issues whatsoever."

"Well, what's at the bottom of them?"

"A bunch of happy travelers!"[42]

"Which slope should we take? The right one, or the left one?"

"I'd take the left slope. I've heard a ton of great things about the left," Good Times said.

Ackshully shifted uncomfortably. "My research clearly shows the right slope is the superior path."

I suppose now is the time to tell you what was at the bottom of each of those slopes. Many eons ago in the Dying Lands, those slopes had led to two different cities. The city to the left was called Grace and had once been a paradise where many travelers had found rest and comfort. Unfortunately, its citizens went mad during a mysterious plague, and the city was burned to the ground. Anyone who took the left slope would find themselves in an ancient ruin filled with man-eating creatures who had once been the inhabitants of the city

[42] There were travelers at the bottom of the slopes, but I can assure you, they were not currently in a state I would describe as "happy."

and end up as an afternoon snack. Which is horrible, of course. Yeah—empathy tells me I should say that's horrible.

The slope on the right led to a city called Truth. It had once been a beacon of peace, strength, and prosperity in the Dying Lands, but over the centuries, it had descended into tyranny and oppression. Anyone who took the slope down to the city of Truth would find themselves enslaved by powerful rulers and forced to live out their remaining years in hard physical labor. Also bad.

The eight single-file travelers on the path began to debate among themselves which way to go. The debate turned into an argument, which got more and more heated as Ryan and Faith watched in silence. Soon, the travelers were screaming in each other's faces. When one of them brandished a pair of shears, seven more shears answered. The argument turned into an all-out brawl, with many wounds inflicted. In the end, the battered group decided to part ways. Three bruised and bloodied travelers dove to the right and slid down the hill, suddenly giggling with glee. The other five held hands and jumped off to the left, whooping and hollering all the way down. Ryan watched as they disappeared into the mist, never to be seen again.[43]

"Well, should we take a slope? Should we try to make it all the way across without sliding down?" he said, turning to Faith.

"Maybe we should look at the Book," said Faith.

Good Times and Ackshully both stifled a giggle.

"Ooooooh, you're one of those?" said Good Times, shaking his head in disappointment.

Ackshully sneered. "Historians have confirmed that Book was written long before this pathway across the slopes was built. You'll find nothing in there to help you," he spat his words. "Besides, do you know how many people that Book has gotten killed?"

---

[43] Well, the human-eating mutants at the bottom of the slope would see them, of course. And that wouldn't end well.

Faith ignored them both and opened the Book to a familiar passage. "It just says 'stay on the path.' Do you think that applies here?"

"Isn't there something a little more clear? Maybe a mention of these slopes that can help us?"

"Nope. Not that I can find."

Well, crap on a stick. Ryan could feel himself getting agitated. Sometimes, the Book came alive with richness and beauty, filling him with assurance and purpose. Other times, it felt frustratingly vague, dry, and unhelpful.

Why couldn't the King have just explicitly told us what to do? It seems like there's no way forward. Are we supposed to just walk down the path and take our chances with the archers?

Apparently having read his mind, Faith spoke up. "I think we need to walk down the path and take our chances with the archers."

"Great!" said Ryan, throwing his hands up. "You first!"

Faith gently put her hand on his arm. "Ryan, I think we just need to trust the King."

"But what if we're wrong? Is this how you want our journey to end? With our heads bursting into a puff of red mist?"

"We may be wrong, it may not end well," she said. "But where else can we go? Who else do we turn to? The King made these lands. The King sent us on this journey. It's not up to us how it ends. It's just up to us to obey the King, and that's it."

"That's it, huh?"

"Yeah . . . I think so. If the King is good, we have to trust He's doing the right thing, whether we live or . . . you know . . . red mist—like you said."

Ryan sighed. He wished that scroll in his pocket could do something useful, like turn into a magic carpet to take them directly to their journey's end. Why did this have to be so hard? He reached in his pocket and felt the tattered edges of the crumpled scroll. He remembered the words, written there in red. He closed his eyes and sighed.

"OK. OK. Let's go. And I'll go first, OK?" Ryan gave Faith a fake reassuring look and could tell she saw right through it. *Welp, I guess this is the end. Red-mist time. Boom. Like when Matt used to beat me in* Halo. *That kid was unnaturally good with the crossbow in* Blood Gulch. He was surprised by the clarity with which he beheld this memory, as most thoughts of his past life had begun to fade like old Polaroids left on a dusty shelf.

His thoughts were interrupted by laughter. He spun around to see Good Times and Ackshully on the ground, laughing hysterically.

"You two have to be the biggest morons I've ever seen!" laughed Ackshully through streaming tears. "If you are stupid enough to believe that Book and walk into a bullet, you deserve to die!"

Good Times interjected. "Come on dudes, you're just joking, I know it, right? Let me get you across the slopes without dying!"

Ryan suddenly felt hesitant again. Being laughed at wasn't fun, especially when he was probably about to die. A part of him wanted to throw his hands up and walk back into the Blackmuck Woods and take his chances with the zombies again. At least right and wrong felt more clear when fighting a pack of murderous zombies. But something in him knew Faith was right. Trusting the King was the only way. So he lifted his right foot and placed it gingerly down on the first paver of the path and winced.

Silence.

He took another step, then another, all the time waiting for the crack of that deadly rifle, which would be the last sound he would ever hear. He turned back to Faith. "Hey, are you coming with me, or not?"

"Of course," she said, gathering her things. "I'm right behind you, Ryan."

Faith held onto Ryan as they took one slow, wincing step at a time down the path. They came to the place where the first in the zombie line had met his, um, "explosive" end. The pavers became slippery as they walked through the giant red mess. All Ryan could think about was how that would be him any second.

"Look up ahead, Ryan."

Ryan lifted his eyes to the far-off peak, miles down the narrow path. The sunset lights of the Golden City seemed to dance and skip across the clouds, although the peak ahead obscured the city itself.

"Just keep your eyes on that light. Walk straight for the mountain. Remember what's beyond it," said Faith as she gripped his arm tightly.

Ryan stopped hunching over and stood straight. He suddenly felt a sense of peace wash over him. Whether he lived or died on this narrow path, he knew he was doing the right thing now.

Then, suddenly, *twang!*

The horrific sound rang out and shattered the silence. Ryan heard a projectile whiz right over his left shoulder. He heard a little girl screaming.

Oh wait—no. That's me, he realized as he heard himself screeching like a maniac.

His survival instinct kicked in and he dove to the right, headfirst over the railing and onto the slippery slope.

"Nope! Not today!" came a voice from behind. A hand firmly grabbed his ankle, preventing him from sliding further. Faith had caught him.

TWHIP. Another arrow whizzed by, sending other travelers careening down the slippery slope to their doom. Ryan's reason soon caught up with his survival instinct and he felt shame. He twisted his body around and clawed his way back up to hold onto the railing. "I got it, Faith. You can let go now, OK?" Ryan felt humiliated. He pulled himself back onto the path. There were no more arrows. All was silent. The two looked at each other—Ryan with shame and Faith with understanding.

"Are you ready to keep going?" said Faith.

"Yeah, I think so."

They resumed their slow walk along the path. Additional shots never came. The only sound was from Good Times and Ackshully, who were still laughing. But as the pair continued to move forward, those laughs faded, and Faith and Ryan were greeted by a view filled with the dancing lights of the Golden City.

CHAPTER 13:

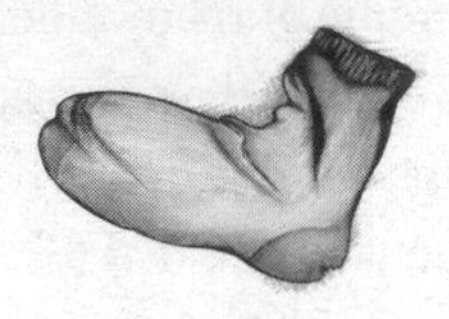

ENDURANCE

The essential thing "in heaven and in earth" is, apparently (to repeat it once more), that there should be long OBEDIENCE in the same direction, there thereby results, and has always resulted in the long run, something which has made life worth living; for instance, virtue, art, music, dancing, reason, spirituality—anything whatever that is transfiguring, refined, foolish, or divine.

—Friedrich Nietzsche, *Beyond Good and Evil*

Ryan and Faith kept walking, and then they walked some more. The path seemed endless, unchanging. They stopped to eat as the sun went down. It was clear to them they would be on this thin stretch of road for days. Even the setting of the sun and the darkness of the sky failed to obscure the brilliance of the city in the distance. They ate dry bread as the sun disappeared behind the misty horizon. With no real room to set up camp, they decided to keep going.

The perpetual sunset of the lights beyond the looming mountain range made them feel some hope, but the peak up ahead never seemed to get closer. In addition to his exhaustion, Ryan began to feel something he hadn't felt since entering the Dying Lands: boredom. The feeling was made worse, of course, by the fact that they weren't alone on these slopes. In every direction, on the right and the left, travelers were continuing to gleefully slide down the hill, on sleds, on skis, on their bellies. There were amusements, refreshments, leisure stations,

all manned by a vendor calling out to them, beckoning them down onto the slope with them. Some of them called out and ridiculed Ryan and Faith. Entire groups of travelers would join in. Other groups watched in nervous anticipation for an archer's head shot that never came. And all the while, the pair plodded forward on the same skinny, sterile path.

There were no vendors or rest stops up on the path with them. Just straight, empty boredom that stretched out into the distance.

Ryan smelled some meat cooking and flashed back to a weird distant dream—or perhaps a memory—of eating a beef patty loaded with lettuce, tomato, and onion at a place called In-N-Out. He could almost taste the animal-style fries,[44] and it began to drive him mad.

"I would die right now for some of the cheese they served back in the City of Destruction," he said, glancing longingly back in the direction they'd come.

"Would you die to see your city flattened by flaming—what were they called—meteorites again?" Faith shot back.

"No, I guess not," sighed Ryan. "But are we really better off now? Here we are starving on this empty path, a bunch of people are laughing at us, and there are sharpshooters preparing to take our heads off at any moment."

"We're closer to the Golden City, though."

Ryan sighed again. It sure didn't feel like they were any closer.

In the darkness they could see the flickering of torches on the slopes, crowds gathered around fires, and hear the laughter of travelers as they slid down into the abyss.

Faith sensed Ryan's discouragement. She opened the Book as she walked and read some passages aloud.

---

[44] Man, I gotta tell you about the animal-style fries. They've got MELTED CHEESE on them. I think I might have mentioned my fascination with cheese. So when you're talkin' melted cheese and grilled onions on those fresh-cut fries topped with some In-N-Out spread . . . ugh, I wish I were a human.

"'Run with endurance the race the King has set before us. Don't turn away from the lights of the city.'"

"'There are far, far better things ahead than any we leave behind.'"

"'So the darkness will be the light—and the stillness, the dancing.'"[45]

Ryan couldn't fully wrap his mind around the words, but found them encouraging, and he felt his body relax at the sound of Faith's gentle voice as she read them. But even as hc found himself getting lost in the words and in Faith's voice, his meditations were punctuated by sharp interruptions.

"'Little things comfort us because little things distress us.'"

My feet hurt.

"'Hope is never ill when Faith is well.'"

I want some cheese.

"'The best prayers often have more groans than words.'"

I'm thirsty.

How much longer?

"Are you distracted?" Faith closed the Book and looked over at him.

"Yeah, I guess." He could feel the sweat on his back growing cold in the night air. His feet were soggy.

Faith stashed the Book and took his arm. "Stop. Sit down for a second." She looked up at him with a smile.

"For what?" Ryan responded.

"Let me take a look at your feet. You may need a change of socks. You know, like the Book says in the passage written by Lieutenant Dan the Great: 'If you're traveling on the road, take care of your feet. Always remember to change your socks!'"

"Huh? No. I'm fine."

---

[45] Faith was once again reading from the Book of Bunyan, which included contributions from the ancient prophets Pascal the Wise, Clive Lewis the Joyful, and Sir Thomas Eliot the Feeble.

Faith stopped as Ryan kept going. He turned to see her with her left hand on her hip, her right finger pointing at the ground, and a glint in her eye. "I'm not taking another step until you sit down!"

"OK, whatever, but I don't see how this—"

"Just relax, Ryan. It will only take a second."

Faith knelt down as Ryan sat. She began untying his shoes. "I can take off my own shoes, Faith, I—"

But Faith shushed him once again.

Faith carefully removed Ryan's worn shoes. He had been sloshing around in them all day, his sweat running from his head, down his back, and into his socks, which were now soaked. Faith peeled them off and threw them aside. If they stank, she didn't let on that she noticed.

"Your feet are a mess!" she exclaimed. "Now, take off that shirt. I have a new tunic for you in my bag."

Ryan obediently removed his soaked shirt and let it fall to the ground with a loud *splock*.

Faith dug through her satchel, singing quietly to herself an ancient tune of the Dying Lands. It was a beautiful, cheerful tune, probably from long ago during better days, before plague and decay had taken the realm. Faith's voice was soft, melodic, and beautiful. Ryan looked down at her. He hadn't really taken the time to notice it before now. Her red hair and fair skin were gorgeous. Her eyes had that glint of fire even as they poured forth compassion. *Who is this girl?*

The singing stopped. "Here we go!"

Faith produced a clean pair of dry socks and a fresh tunic from her bag. She also produced one of the last pieces of bread from the city of Evangelion. "Here, eat up. I'm not even hungry."

Ryan started to protest, but Faith gave him a look that seemed to say: *Don't you even start!* The look was all at once playful, gentle, and brimming with kindness. He took the bread and ate gratefully.

Faith resumed her singing as she unrolled the socks and pulled them up around Ryan's feet and up his ankles. As he put on his new shirt, she turned his boots upside down, dumping sticks, dirt, and pebbles out onto the cold stone pavers.

"Hey, uh, Faith?"

"Yeah?"

"Thanks."

She said nothing, only looking up to smile at him. She tenderly pushed his boots back onto his feet and began to cinch the laces to the top, ending with a strong knot.

Then, instead of beckoning him to stand up and get going again, she took a spot on the path beside him and sat down, her head resting on his shoulder, and began to softly sing again. Ryan felt himself getting lost in it—transported by its haunting beauty as it rose and fell and made him forget his aching muscles and weariness.

After a while, Faith's voice trailed off and she looked up at him again. "So . . . you ready to keep going?"

Ryan was a new man. He wasn't just ready to keep going, he was ready to storm a castle.

And so they kept going. I won't bore you with a detailed description of their journey. Honestly, not much happened. Just a long, tedious trek forward on a very straight and narrow path. I mean—I had to sit through the whole thing, which wasn't easy. It's part of my job as The Narrator. I get no fast-forward button. But Faith and Ryan had to live through it. Several days on an unforgiving pathway, temptations on either side. Through it all, I found myself with a newfound awe for the weak, limited image-bearers, and the grace given to them by the Creator to accomplish far more than they should be able to. Tedious to watch, but impressive, nonetheless. Faith's gentle singing helped pass the time. I found myself longing to know her story, to find out where such a gentle, delightful creature came from. I haven't been given access to her files, though. But that voice of hers . . . you could tell her story could fill a bookshelf.

CHAPTER 14:

PARADOX PEAK

Because [the cross] has a paradox in its center it can grow without changing. The circle returns upon itself and is bound. The cross opens its arms to the four winds; it is a signpost for free travelers.

—G. K. Chesterton, *Orthodoxy*

Humans sometimes eat this thing called "meatloaf," and it's unclear to me why. It's ketchup mashed up with onions and processed cow meat that was deemed unfit for steaks or burgers. There may be good meatloaf somewhere in the multiverse, but I haven't found it yet. Why humans eat the stuff remains a mystery to me, whose wandering eye searches out all enigmas and riddles concerning mankind. I've contemplated the problem of evil and the justice of God, and still. Meatloaf. What's the deal with meatloaf?

All that to say, Ryan and Faith's ragged, bloody, and blistered feet reminded me of meatloaf: shredded and oozing. (Is that gross? Sorry if that's gross. I'm trying some things out you humans call "imagery" and "simile.")

Anyway, they arrived at long last at the foot of the peak that had been growing nearer and nearer every day without seeming to. There's something psychologically draining about hiking for days, beating your body black and blue, dragging yourself along over obstacle after obstacle, when you know you have the greatest challenge looming closer all the time. So it was something of a relief to our pilgrims to have arrived. At least it would be over soon, one way or the other.

The peak rose 8,862 feet in front of them. The Road cut into the mountainside, weaving in and out of sharp boulders and along precarious precipices. To their left, some twenty miles in the distance, the dusty red cliffs of the Great Plateau joined with the mountain range. To their right, dense woods and thickets climbed up impossibly tall heights. In short, the Road was the only way forward.

"Well," Ryan sighed, "might as well get on with it. I don't see any way around. And we've learned our lesson not to leave the Road. At least I hope we have."

Faith winced and plopped down on a boulder at the start of the trail that cut into the mountainside. "Owwwww," she said as she took off her boots and shook several rocks out of them. "You don't see a tavern around this place, do you? I know we have to stick to the Road. But I sure could use a rest. And a beer."

Ryan looked around. "I don't think many people come this way, Faith."

Everything before them looked wild, unkempt, deserted. Dark clouds churned overhead, swirling around the top of the peak. A bird on a skeletal tree cawed, echoing against the cold, dead rock.

"Well, up and over, I guess," Faith sighed. They started up the switchbacks. The slope was gradual at first. It felt good to them to have gotten started, at least, as it always does when one finally starts a task one has been dreading, like mowing the lawn or writing a book.

The cool of the morning gave way to brutal midday. The sun crested the peak above them—dark, mystical cloud notwithstanding—and began to beat down hard, testing their endurance and resolve.

—

"Ryan, look—the view!" Faith said suddenly, hours and hours later. They were roughly halfway up the mountain, huffing and puffing and wiping grimy sweat from their brows. Ryan turned, and what he saw both stunned him and filled him with dread. Behind them, the road wound back into the distance. They could make out the dark forest, a glint of sunlight reflecting off Evangelion's glass dome, now a speck in the distance—and just beyond that, there was nothing but fire and death.

Brimstone from the heavens rained down like hail, decimating everything that lay beneath. The horizon was on fire, and smoke slowly drifted up to the sky.

"It's started, then," Faith said. "The end of all things. The end of my world."

They watched in silence for a while. Ryan looked over to see Faith was crying. "It's strange," she said at last. "All my life I've been trying to get out of this place, and yet I find in some weird way I love it after all. And the only thing I can do to save it is to leave it, is to walk forward. There's no magic spell, no battle to be won, no final confrontation with the big bad evil guy. Just me and you walking the road as the world burns around us."

They watched a while longer and then reluctantly trudged on up the mountain.

The evening sun had begun to dip toward the horizon when they heard a low rumbling to their right, up the slope of the peak. Ryan's eyes shot up just in time to see a slew of jagged, broken boulders hurtling toward them.

"Rockslide!" he cried, though he remained frozen to the spot. Faith was quicker on her feet and grabbed him, pulling him behind a stump just in time. They sat with their backs to it, wincing as boulders slammed into the crooked, creaking tree stump just behind them, covering them in dust and gravel. Finally, the storm subsided, and Ryan dared to poke his head out. The rockslide had covered hundreds of feet of the slope, wiping out much of the trail.

"Great," he muttered, dusting himself off and helping Faith up. "Looks like we'll have to climb straight up for a while."

"Ow," said Faith, and Ryan saw she'd been scraped by a falling rock, opening up a gash along her Hollowplague-ridden arm. She winced.

"I don't suppose there's another one of those healer guys around here anywhere," Ryan said, shielding his eyes from the dust as he looked up and around.

"He was, like, a demon," she reminded him.

"Yeah, but I did get healed," he said. "You can't be too picky when you're injured in the middle of nowhere, I guess."

She gave him a wry smile and started up the hillside.

After a half hour or so of difficult work picking a path across the haphazard patchwork of fallen boulders, they found the path again, cutting horizontally across the face of the mountain. It appeared to be where the rockslide started.

They froze. There, on a rock on the side of the path, was a smiley face drawn in blood.

That night, they camped in a small clearing, being careful to stay within eyesight of the path itself. What rations they had left from Evangelion were dwindling, but Faith said they should have enough to last them until the River Infinite.

The night passed clear and cold and gave way to a bright and blistering morning sun. The path had wrapped around the south side of the mountain at this point, exposing them to its brutal rays as they continued to work their way up the unforgiving sheet of rock. They set off just after dawn, wanting to get as much of the Road as possible behind them before the real heat of the day set in.

"What I wouldn't do for a Klondike Bar right now," Ryan said, not really remembering very well what a Klondike Bar was nor why he wanted one.

Faith didn't seem to hear, or didn't care, and pressed on a few paces ahead of him, leading him up countless switchbacks until the sun beat down on their faces, their backs ached, and their feet looked more and more like that infernal thing called "meatloaf."

Eventually, Ryan encountered a strange phenomenon: his body was willing to press on, but his mind protested with every step. He was so worn and beaten and bruised that his body was numb to most of the pain, and whatever aches and sores did manage to stab through to his consciousness, he actually welcomed on some level. It felt good to get out and *do* something, to press on to complete a journey. He hadn't had that experience before, as just about everything he took up, he'd give up just as quickly. To feel the pain that came with pressing on toward a distant goal was invigorating.

And yet, his mind protested. It wasn't his body that wanted to slow down, take another rest, take it easy. It was his will. His mind begged him to stop even as his body told him it could yet go further. The challenge was not in taking the next step—not really. Not in a physical sense, anyway. The challenge was in willing himself to take the next step. It was in wanting to take the next step, and in *wanting* to want to take the next step.

Faith looked back. "Are you alright?"

Ryan snapped out of his thoughts and managed a pitiable smile. "Yes. Just trying to force myself to put one foot in front of the other."

She turned and pressed on. Just her company had a motivating effect on Ryan. Watching someone else take the next step is sometimes all the encouragement you need to take it yourself.

As they rounded a bend that took them into the cool shade of the west side of the mountain once again, a bizarre sight awaited them. Lining both sides of the path were people—or what looked like people—standing silently and watching them. They stood on each side of the path, evenly spaced, several rows deep, their eyes following like quiet guardians.

They were Hollow Ones. Their cold blue eyes stared ahead. They were there and yet not there, empty, transparent shells of who they once had been. They said nothing as Ryan and Faith approached. The path flattened out here onto a kind of shelf or plateau before it rose sharply into the final climb to the summit a hundred yards ahead.

"I don't like this," Faith said quietly, her eyes darting wildly from side to side at their watchers.

"I've seen enough horror movies to know this doesn't end well," Ryan responded. "Horror movies, see, are these . . ." his voice trailed off as he tried to recall what horror movies were.

Then, just behind them, they heard footsteps approaching. The unnatural rockslide and the smiley face and who might have drawn it jumped into Ryan's mind. He automatically reached for his sword but grasped only air, having forgotten that it had shattered—a terribly constructed weapon. In the meantime, Faith had drawn her sword and stood with it already prepared. Their backs were now to the watchers as they stood waiting to see who would come around the bend.

They were surprised to see a normal, happy, smiling pilgrim skipping up the path and whistling some vaguely familiar tune.[46] He clutched his Book against his side; a sword was upon his back.

[46] It was "Oceans," which is ostensibly one of your human worship songs on Earth. I've listened to it several times and still can't figure out what in the world it's about.

"Greetings, fellow pilgrims!" he said, introducing himself as Mr. Loved-by-the-World.

"Hi," said Ryan. "Not sure you're going to like what's ahead."

The pilgrim surveyed the staring watchers, meeting their unbroken gazes.

"Surely it's not as bad as you think," he said. "I'll go first. The Hollow Ones are just misunderstood, you see. They're not so bad once you get to know them."

"They're basically zombies," Ryan replied.

"Now, don't go talking like that," Mr. Loved-by-the-World scolded. "The Hollow Ones will never like you if you go on using that kind of language."

"The Hollow Ones hate all pilgrims," Faith replied. "It's right here in the Book. 'Unless they be chosen and transformed by the King Himself, the Hollow Ones will hate you. They hate the King, and you are followers of the King; therefore, you will be hated by all who inhabit the Dying Lands. Seek not their love nor attention.'"

"Well, amen and amen!" Mr. Loved-by-the-World replied. "I agree with every word of the Book, of course. And yet . . . and yet my heart tells me differently. There's some nuance there, you see. It can't mean exactly what it says. It would be unloving to think that we can't like and be liked by the world."

And with that, Mr. Loved-by-the-World merrily pressed on into the gauntlet between the lines of silent watchers.

Suddenly, the Hollow Ones sprang to life. "Go back," they said in unison. "You're going the wrong way."

Mr. Loved-by-the-World stopped and turned, addressing the crowd.

"Greetings, O Misunderstood Ones!" he shouted. "I am but a simple pilgrim making my way to the Golden City. You are welcome to join me, for it is a smart thing to do to make for the Golden City. All the smartest scholars and bravest knights of our land are doing it."

"Go back," they replied. "The way is too hard."

"Oh, I do love a good dialogue with you folks!" he said. "Very well. I have here an article I've written for the *Evangelion Daily Herald* entitled 'Seven Reasons You Should Make For the Golden City.' Shall I read it for you?"

"Go back," they replied. "Join us."

What followed was a twenty-seven-minute-long conversation between Mr. Loved-by-the-World and the Hollow Ones, and it was quite dull. I shall not chronicle it for you here, or else you might grow bored of this book and read something else. And I really want you to get to the end of this story. It's a good one. Anyway, he continued to try to persuade them with reason and facts, and they continued to tell him to go back.

At the end of the conversation, Mr. Loved-by-the-World merrily skipped back toward Ryan and Faith.

"What are you doing?" Ryan asked. "Now you're going backward."

"Yes, but the Hollow Ones love me!" he said. "They say they approve of this direction. They pointed out it was much smarter and more socially acceptable to go *downhill* instead of *uphill*, which is much more difficult."

"But that way leads to only destruction and death," Faith said. "Only by going forward can we get to the Golden City."

"Yes, but then some people *won't like us*," Mr. Loved-by-the-World said. "I can handle a dark, scary forest. I can handle an uphill climb. I could have made it across the rushing waters of the River Infinite. What I can't deal with is people not liking me. It's awkward and uncomfortable. I'm heading back, and I suggest you do the same."

With that, he was gone, back toward fire and death.

Ryan and Faith stepped forward. There was no more putting it off: it was time to face the watchers.

They stepped into the narrow way between the silently watching Hollow Ones. As soon as they did so, the Hollows responded. "Go back," they said. "The way is too hard."

Some magical effect must have been in play, because Ryan immediately wanted to go back. More than that, he wanted to entertain their discussion and argue with their reasoning. "But the Book tells us to go this way," he responded, his mind slowly being overtaken by some kind of fog.

"The Book lies," they whispered. "Why would a good and loving King ask you to do something so difficult? So impossible? That way lies your doom."

"That way . . . that way lies our salvation," Ryan said at last with great effort. He took another step, the weight of the watchers' words burdening him further and further. He looked frantically around for Faith. She was just in front of him but didn't seem to notice, as she herself was arguing with the watchers as well. Ryan was brought to his knees. The voices of the watchers seemed to amplify themselves and overlap one another. "Go back. You're a fool. Go back to safety. Go back to comfort. Join us. Join us. Join us."

His mind was overtaken with their words. But some vague remembrance suddenly pierced his thoughts. Lying face-down in the dirt, he fumbled for his pockets. Out came the Book. He opened to a random page.[47]

"'The King is my guide, I shall not want anything,'" he said weakly. "'He makes me rest beside the Road, he leads me to drink of still waters.'"

The Hollow Ones hissed and stepped back.

"'He restores my heart and helps me to press on toward the . . . the Golden City.'"

---

[47] Nothing, of course, is truly random, but I use the term for your human understanding.

They hissed again and took another step back. Ryan's mind began to clear. He looked up and saw Faith prone on the ground muttering to herself. "Must go back. No way forward. Too hard. This is foolish. Foolish. Foolish."

Ryan stumbled over to her and pulled her up.

"Say it with me, Faith!" He opened the book and shoved it in her face.

She numbly recited with him. "'Thy scepter and staff, they comfort me.'" The Hollow Ones were in a full scream now, reaching forward, though some good magic kept them from stepping onto the Road.

"'Yea, though I walk through the shadow of the Mountain of Death, I will fear no evil.'" Their voices were getting stronger now, and the Hollow Ones were beginning to break formation, buckling before the words of the Book. "'You prepare me a feast in the presence of the Hollow Ones. You anoint me with oil. My cup is filled with delicious wine.'

"'Surely I will dwell in the Golden City from now until the very reaches of eternity!'"

With this last cry, the Hollow Ones fled, scurrying back to whatever cave or hole they came from. Faith and Ryan were alone once more. They collapsed into each other's arms and rested.

It's a funny thing, getting to the top of a mountain. What seemed so distant and unattainable suddenly seems as though it were inevitable all along, as though it were the most natural thing in the world to simply climb eight thousand feet into the air. One minute, Ryan was struggling up the rocky cliff face, the path barely visible among the treacherous rocks; the next, he was standing triumphantly on the top of Paradox Peak.

On top of the peak stood a wooden cross. Its paradoxical intersection of two simple wooden beams seemed out of place in the middle of the random and chaotic natural world they found themselves in, and yet there it stood, resolute, unchanging, equal parts definite and infinite, immediate and eternal. Ryan had a vague memory of this symbol in his own world, though its exact meaning escaped him at the moment. It at once brought back feelings of hope, love, beauty, despair, anger, pain, and suffering. He hated it and loved it all at once.

To their right was a deep crack in the earth, dropping to the very heart of the mountain itself. Whatever unknown depths it fell to were miles and miles beneath them, maybe as deep as eternity. Ryan took a few steps toward the crack and looked down. There was nothing—blackness, emptiness. Not sure what he was doing, Ryan picked up a small rock. Memories came rushing upon him. Things he had done. People he had hurt. Regrets. Visions of himself wasting his life—in a meaningless parade of entertainment, pleasure, anything to numb the pain—came washing over him. He saw a dark, lonely soul. Hollow. Trudging through a meaningless life toward nothing—no purpose, no end goal, no epic finale. He saw himself drowning in a bog, wasting his life in a city full of apathetic pilgrims, straying off the path again and again and again. He felt the impossible pressure of his failures weighing down on him like a great burden strapped to his back. And he saw a Man dying on a cross, falling into the darkness, and emerging again triumphant.

He idly tossed the rock down the chasm. He never heard it hit the bottom.

He wasn't sure what had just happened, but Ryan felt curiously light, as though a burden he'd been weighed down with all his life had been loosened and had fallen down the chasm with the rock.

"Ryan, look!" Faith said, interrupting his appointment with eternity.

"What is it?" he said numbly, still adrift in his thoughts.

"The Golden City!"

Ryan glanced away from the cross and in her direction, and sure enough, there it was. The pain of his feet and the aching of his legs did not seem to be worth comparing to the sight he saw now, distant though it was. The landscape in front of him was dry, cracked, and bare, something out of a Clint Eastwood Western.[48] Rocky crags and bluffs broke up the deserted landscape, and what looked like a settlement or two dotted the land stretched out before them. The Road wove like a thread through the land, a line of certainty in the world of chaos all around them.

But beyond that, past a mighty rushing river of blackness, they could see it: a city of gold. Its towers seemed impossibly high, brushing the very heavens. They could not, of course, behold its glory in its entirety from the Dying Lands themselves: there was a kind of shroud or fog over it, and yet it was unmistakably there for any who would turn their eyes upon its golden gates and towering walls of brass, silver, and steel. One thing Ryan had not expected was how infinite it looked. It appeared to have a clear end point, solid walls defining its borders, and yet the more you looked the more unsure you were about that. The more you stared at the Golden City, the more it zoomed in on itself, looking like a never ending well of streets, buildings, towers, parapets, and sparkling roofs of splendor. It was like an eternal kaleidoscope of gold and silver and colors he couldn't even name.

Ryan felt fingers slipping into his. Not in a weird, awkward, junior-high-couple-holding-hands-at-the-school-dance kind of way. Not really even in a romantic way. Just in a way that felt like the most natural thing in the world. Ryan gripped Faith's hand back. They looked down into the valley, the Golden City lit up by the crimson afternoon sun.

"We're almost there," Ryan said, feeling a sense of hope for the first time in many weeks.

---

[48] Reference to your human movies.

"And yet, we have a long way to go," Faith said.

They started down the mountain, the end of their journey in sight.

Behind them, peering out from the shadows of a scraggly tree on the other side of the fissure, a bald man in a suit lit a cigarette, took a long, slow draw, and smiled a hollow smile. He snapped his fingers and ripped a hole in time and space.

CHAPTER 15:

THE VALLEY OF DOUBT

It is during such trough periods, much more than during the peak periods, that it is growing into the sort of creature He wants it to be . . . He wants them to learn to walk and must therefore take away His hand; and if only the will to walk is really there He is pleased even with their stumbles.

—C. S. Lewis, *The Screwtape Letters*

Inching down the mountain wasn't any easier than climbing up. Their meatloaf feet had further dissolved into something even more unrecognizable, sending sharp, shooting pain up their legs with each step. Before them, the path was littered with sharp rocks and fallen trees, twisting like a broken arm as it led to a yawning canyon below. Soon, they would be in the dark and unable to see the Golden City.

"And here I was, thinking the hard part was over," Ryan said aloud. "Silly me."

Faith gave him a look. It wasn't a chiding look, but a look of understanding. "I know," she said simply. Then she fell silent.

As they trudged ahead, they saw a kind of clearing had opened up on their right. An unkempt lawn had been cut into the forest, with varied stumps still protruding from the grass. On one of the stumps sat a man. He was extraordinarily fat and sported a scraggly beard that was about as well-kept as the grass surrounding him, and on his head was a strange-looking hat. I would say the hat most closely resembled what you call a "fedora" in your world.

In front of him was a large rock that formed a sort of makeshift desk, for he was furiously writing on a scroll atop the rock. Behind him was a large cage full of sparrows that pecked at scattered seed within, and beyond was the opening of a dark cave cut into the hillside. The man looked up from his writing and sneered at the pilgrims as they walked by.

"What are you writing?" Ryan asked, his curiosity defeating his better judgment in a brief internal wrestling match.

"I'm kind of surprised you haven't heard of me, actually. The name's Mr. Neckbeard. I'm kind of a famous arguer here in the Dying Lands. So, I'm arguing," he said proudly, folding his arms. "I maintain regular correspondence with followers of the King. You might say I'm something of an expert on the King. I study everything to do with the King and pilgrims and the Road. I know everything there is to know about the King, the Golden City, you name it. I have dedicated my life to studying Him!"

"So you're a follower of the King, then?" asked Ryan.

"HA!" The man stood up, knocking over his inkpot. "How dare you! I wouldn't follow the King if He appeared right in front of me this very instant! He doesn't even exist!"

Faith and Ryan exchanged a glance. "Uh . . . then why do you spend so much time thinking about Him?" she asked.

"BECAUSE I HATE HIM!" the man cried, turning red in the face. "He's a deceiver and a liar and He abuses gullible travelers who search for Him! Um—I mean, He would do those things if He existed. But He doesn't. Therefore, I spend every waking moment trying to convince followers they're being lied to. Besides, you can still follow the Road without believing in the King. People do it all the time."

"How can you not believe in the King?" Faith asked, her curiosity piqued in spite of herself. "Who do you think built the Road, then?"

"ACTUALLY, the accepted consensus among people outside the bubble of Evangelion is that it arose by natural processes. Over millions of years, a river carved out the road. Any appearance of design is completely coincidental."

"That's insane," Ryan said. "Some of it is even paved with cobblestones, clearly carved by something or Someone."

"To the normie, sure, you can believe that some all-powerful magic 'King' created the Road. But we free-thinkers know better. If you leave enough stones sitting around for enough time, it's inevitable that they'll form into a road."

"OK, sure. You go ahead and believe that," Faith replied. "But even so—we can literally see the Golden City right over the horizon there. You can't deny that it exists."

"Ah, so young, so simple-minded," Mr. Neckbeard scoffed. He waved his hand. "A simple trick of light refracting through the atmosphere. It's an optical illusion. Only the very young or very stupid still believe that there's some magical place of peace and happiness where the King lives over the River Infinite. Once we cross the River, there's nothing but blackness."

"I mean, the evidence is pretty overwhelming that it's right there," Ryan said. "I can literally see it. It seems like you're the one who's simple-minded."

"I see through the trick!" Neckbeard insisted, getting red in the face again. "You just see the surface. I see through things. In fact, I see through everything! I can see that in the end, nothing really matters! Nothing matters! NOTHING MATTERS!!!"

"You're pretty passionate about this belief of yours that nothing matters," Faith said.

"Ah, but once you realize there is no pretend 'Golden City' and no King, everything actually matters more, because only what we do here in the Dying Lands lasts," he responded. "You fools can simply do whatever you want in this life, in the delusional belief that in this mythical city all will be made right one day."

"But in practice, that's just not true. I've devoted my life to helping others," Faith said. "You are sitting here arguing with people you don't even know."

"I'm helping them out of their ignorance," Neckbeard snapped. "This is important work. I want everyone to know how much I don't care about this 'King' of yours who does not exist."

Mr. Neckbeard stood up and stroked his, well, neckbeard. He signed the scroll he was working on with a flourish, rolled it up, and walked over toward his birdcage. Pulling out one of the sparrows, he tied the scroll to its foot and released it into the sky.[49]

"There," he said. "Another missive sent. Another pilgrim possibly saved from a life of delusion."

"Well, good luck to you, I guess," Ryan said. "We'd best be on our way."

"HE DOES NOT EXIST!" Mr. Neckbeard screamed suddenly.

Ryan and Faith jumped back, startled.

"HE DOES NOT EXIST!" he continued. "HE DOES NOT EXIST!" Mr. Neckbeard stared out at the Golden City, taking it all in. And then, he started clawing at his face, scratching at his own eyes. "HE DOES NOT EXIST!" Bloody scratches formed on his face.

"Dude!" Ryan cried. "You're hurting yourself!"

Mr. Neckbeard ran into his cave. Ryan and Faith chased after him.

"He doesn't exist! HE DOES NOT! EXIST! HE! DOES! NOT! EXIST!!! AHHHHHHHH!!!"

[49] These message-carrying sparrows are the main means of long-distance communication in the Dying Lands, enabling people to scream and argue to their hearts' content with people they've never met. I can't imagine why anyone would waste their life doing that. Where I come from, the birds are there simply for beauty and song. They write some of the best Hymns too. If I wasn't trying to wrap up this story, I'd translate one for you now.

Glancing within, they saw Mr. Neckbeard with a piece of chalk, frantically scrawling the word "DARKNESS" on the inside of his cave. "I WILL BLOT OUT THE LIGHTS OF THE CITY! I WILL BLOT OUT THE LIGHTS OF THE CITY!" he cried over and over and over again.

"I don't think we can help him," Faith whispered, taking Ryan's hand. "We'd better get moving."

As they turned to exit the cave, they were stopped cold by Neckbeard's voice as he called out to them from the darkness. He was suddenly calm. His words shed their sneering edge. His tone softened.

"The King's Road . . . is littered with the bodies of people who believed in Him with all their hearts, as you do," he said. "And what did it get them? Pain? Suffering? Death? For what? Who wrote that Book you're carrying, anyway? Do you even know? You think the King has a special mission for you, just because someone wrote that in the pages of an old Book you found under your mattress in the City of Destruction, just as I did?"

Ryan and Faith felt their hearts catch in their throats.

"I took the journey too, you know." Neckbeard had tears in his eyes now. "I followed the road. I lost my friends. I suffered and persevered. I entered the valley that sits before you now. The further I walked, the more I realized I had suffered needlessly. Don't look for meaning in the words of some ancient Book. Look for meaning in the here and now. This right here is what matters."

Faith and Ryan were silent for a moment.

"But . . . the words in the ancient Book are true. We know it," said Faith quietly. Her voice was barely a whisper.

"NO THEY'RE NOT!" Neckbeard screamed, his face beet-red once again.

"And the city is real!" said Ryan. "You can see it yourself!"

"AAAAAAAAA!" Neckbeard screamed, and lunged for Faith, swinging her around, causing her bag to fall off her arm and onto the cave floor. Faith wrested herself away from his grasp and picked up the bag.

"Hey! Take it easy, man!" Ryan yelled, squaring up for a fight.

Neckbeard shrank away, and with a whimper began clawing at his eyes once again.

Ryan and Faith turned again to leave the cave. They heard Neckbeard screaming after them. "YOU FOOLS! If you aren't killed in that valley, you'll be back here with me, and maybe you'll finally be thinking rationally! Only you'll be bruised, bloody, dismembered! You'll waste your life!"

Ryan felt Faith clutch his arm tightly, as if to say: *Let's go.*

And out they walked. Ryan quietly wondered if they would be back here soon, looking up at Mr. Neckbeard as he said, "I told you so!"

The light blinded them momentarily as they exited the cave. They left the clearing, walking past the scattered stumps and Mr. Neckbeard's house, and finally found the path once again.

"You ready?" said Ryan.

Faith flashed a smile. "Of course I am!"

"Well, you sure seem confident."

"The Book is true, Ryan. It just is."

Back on the path, the pair looked out on the imposing landscape before them.

The canyon itself was a starkly contrasting crack in a flat and barren desert that surrounded it. There were no rivers leading in or out. It looked as if a mad giant had struck the earth again and again with some hulking axe fit for a Greek titan. As far as the eye could see, there was no vegetation. Ryan thought he could see creatures skittering around in the shadows of the canyon, where the light of the Golden City couldn't reach. He gulped.

This next part was hard for me, The Narrator, to watch. Remember how I told you earlier that I'm authorized to speak and mildly interfere with events in order to keep our hero on the right path? Well, I wasn't allowed this time. Really frustrating. It felt like I was watching one of those horror movies you people seem to love, but I was just shouting at the screen as the killer crept up behind his blissfully unaware victims. As Ryan and Faith began the trek into the dark valley, neither noticed they had forgotten something. On the ground of the cave, tattered and torn and bound with leather, lay the Book.

They had forgotten the Book!

So now I had to watch these poor souls trudging miles down the hill and into the dark canyon without the King's Book. Climbing over thousands of sharp, loose rocks with messed-up feet takes a while. By the time they made it to the bottom of the deep valley, they had no idea how long they had walked. They didn't know the time, since the sun and the sky and the light of the city were out of view.

I'm not allowed to see the future. I'm just a narrator. But I'll admit at this point that I was worried about what would happen to these two. I'm powerful enough to have helped them, but I wasn't given permission. I started to think that maybe I was assigned the narration of a tragedy in the making—a horrible tale of suffering and defeat that would serve as a warning to others.

Ryan and Faith looked half dead. Their clothes were soaked with sweat. Their arms and legs were covered in blood and bruises. They stood for a moment, on level ground for the first time, surrounded by darkness and skittering shadows. They weren't alone.

"Oh no . . ." Faith realized something was missing from her bag.

"What's wrong?"

"OH NO!" she cried.

Ryan had never heard that kind of desperation in her voice before.

"Where is it? Where is it?" Faith collapsed on the ground and dumped out her bag. "No, no, no, NO!"

Ryan's heart stopped as he realized what Faith was looking for. The Book, with its warm light and words of truth, the very thing they needed to get through this dark place, was gone.

Before either of them could say anything, a screech rang out through the valley, followed by another one. The skittering shadows came to life as pale, emaciated creatures sprang from behind rocks and came bounding toward them. Ryan quickly realized they were humans, or rather, whatever a human becomes after being hollow for a very long time. None of them had hair. They wore tattered clothes that hung off their skeletal frames. Some wore no clothes at all.

"REEEEEEEEEEE!" they screeched as they fell upon the travelers and began to beat them. Their already broken bodies fell easily under the flurry of fists and claws and clubs. It didn't take much for Ryan and Faith to lose consciousness.

I'll admit I was surprised Ryan had made it that far. In your world, he was still an unimpressive guy, but he'd won me over a bit in the course of this journey—or rather—the Creator won me over. The Creator is a great Storyteller, and the people He chooses are so often different than who I would have chosen. He never fails to surprise me.

All that to say, I was really rooting for Ryan and Faith at that point, and I was sad to realize this story might not end well for them. But I kept watching, hoping I was wrong.

When Ryan woke up, he found he was being dragged across the rocky valley floor.

He craned his neck to the side and saw Faith was in the same predicament. Bony, clammy fingers gripped their ankles and dragged them down the road. They came to a clearing full of metal cages. Some were empty; many held skeletons. The hollow creatures dragged Ryan up to one rusty enclosure. Above the door was a placard reading "DESPAIR."

Ryan was roughly tossed into the cage and the door was slammed behind him. Faith, still unconscious, was thrown into another cage across the path. With a chorus of hyena-like laughter, the Hollow Ones scurried away, back into the shadows, leaving the two pilgrims to die.

Ryan looked around at the cages. Each one had a placard above the door, with words like "FRAUD," "LIAR," "FAILURE," and "GULLIBLE". The placard above Faith's frail, unconscious body read, "WEAK."

Time passed. It was impossible to tell how much time, in this place where the sun didn't reach. It could have been hours—to Ryan it felt like days. The valley was cold despite the complete absence of wind. All was silent and dark. Ryan looked around at his cage. It seemed solid, inescapable. In his heart he knew that no one would come for them, just like no one came for the other faithful travelers, now little more than brittle skeletons in their enclosures. Faith still lay there, motionless.

Time flowed on, and Ryan began to despair.

Neckbeard was right, he thought to himself, barely able to believe what he was thinking. This was a mistake, or some sort of terrible trap. *What kind of a King would write a Book that leads hopeful fools to their painful, lonely deaths?*

Ryan forgot the journey, the Book, and Faith. He collapsed on the floor of his cold cage and wept silently and bitterly. *There is no King. There is no Golden City.*

Then his thoughts were interrupted by the words of the Book.

Faith was awake now, her gentle voice carrying across the still air. She was quoting the Book from memory.

"'Your words I have hid in my heart.'"

"'Consider it joy when you face trials, knowing your testing will bring patience and completeness.'"

"'I remain confident in this, that I will see the goodness of the King in the land of the living.'"

"In this world you may have trouble, but take heart, I have overcome the world.'"

"'The King will never leave you or forsake you.'"

The words continued to roll off her tongue as she recited passage after passage to herself. Her voice sounded firm, confident, yet completely at peace.

But to Ryan, they rang hollow. *Some good these words are doing us now,* he thought. He crumpled the tiny scroll in his pocket.

"Walk Forward."

Seriously? To be used in the hour of my greatest need?

Maybe the wisest thing to do now was admit he had been lied to. He could only hope that Mr. Neckbeard would have compassion and come looking for them in the valley.

"You may as well stop quoting the Book, Faith. No one's coming for us. We're gonna die here."

Faith looked at him with weary sadness in her green eyes. "The Book is true, and the King is real, Ryan. I don't know how we'll get out of this, but I can't give up my belief in the King."

Ryan felt Mr. Neckbeard's rage boiling up in him as his face turned red. Everything Faith was saying seem so incredibly stupid now.

Faith spoke the words of the Book again. "Trust in the King with all your heart, and lean not on your own understanding. In all your ways acknowledge Him, and He will make your paths straight. Do not be wise in your own eyes."

Ryan felt conflicted. Never had such comforting words so conflicted with his present circumstances, at least never in this world. His thoughts were interrupted.

"Hey, are you two OK? Are you alive?" A man's voice came from down the dark path. Ryan looked up to see a middle-aged man walking toward them. The man was well dressed, wearing nice slacks and a kind of sweater vest over a collared shirt. He had gray hair somewhat haphazardly combed over the top of his head and a pair of black-framed glasses perched on his nose.

By that point Ryan had learned to suspect everything and everyone he met on the road—especially in this evil place. He half expected this professor-looking guy to transform into a troll or a dragon and eat them both. The man must have sensed Ryan's fear because he quickly said, "Oh no, don't worry! I'm not going to hurt you, I'm here to help! Do you two need medical attention?"

"Are you a traveler for the King?" asked Faith.

"Well, no, I'm not, but who says I need to be a follower of the King to show some human decency and help two poor souls out?" The man's voice was kind, and so were his eyes. "I'm sorry, I didn't introduce myself," he said as he approached them. "My name is Humanist. Let's get you out of these cages."

"Thank you," Ryan managed. Faith still looked skeptical.

Humanist took a look at the cages. "Um, the cages should be unlocked. You may have to jiggle the rusty doors a bit, but you should be able to just open them and walk out."

"Are you kidding?" Ryan shook the door to his cage and sure enough, with a bit of effort, it creaked open. He ran over to Faith and helped her push open her door as well.

"Don't wait around for people to save you. That's what the other ones did," said Humanist, motioning to the skeletons in the other cages. "You have more power and agency than you think you have. Now come along—let's get you some medical attention."

"Where are you from?" said Faith, still skeptical.

"I'm from down here! The city of Urbia. There's a whole community of people down here who have managed to find meaning and purpose in the Valley. It's an oasis. Someday, the towers of the city will rise above the Valley and be a new beacon for travelers like yourself. Doubt doesn't have to be a bad thing, you know. Once you come to terms with reality, it really frees you up to do good for others simply because they're human, instead of because a Book told you to."

"What reality?" asked Ryan.

"Oh—well, the fact that there is no King and no Golden City. I know what you're gonna say, but trust me. I've been to the end of this valley and seen the other side. There's no city. Just endless desert. I'm really sorry. That can't be easy to hear. Especially after all you've been through. We'll talk later. For now, let's just get to the city of Urbia. Are you able to walk a bit longer?"

Ryan could tell Faith wanted to object, but she said nothing. She instead gripped his arm and leaned on him as they followed Humanist.

They rounded a bend in the road and were suddenly bathed in light. Up ahead loomed Urbia, whose lights seemed to shine brighter than those of the Golden City.

CHAPTER 16:

URBIA

Barbarism is the natural state of mankind . . . Civilization is unnatural. It is a whim of circumstance. And barbarism must always ultimately triumph.

—Robert E. Howard, *Beyond the Black River*

When Faith walked into the twilight-tinged outskirts of Urbia holding tight to Ryan's arm, she could not, of course, have known that in just five hours she would take her last breath.

Dang, spoilers again. Was that bad? Sorry.

The city was unlike anything she had ever seen. Rows and rows of pristine, identical wooden houses lined the street, which was paved with a black, rocky substance and painted with weird white and yellow lines. Every once in a while, they would walk by a strange yellow box lined with lights that would alternately shine red, green, and yellow. On a street corner she saw a furry four-legged creature panting and relieving himself on a yellow, cylindrically shaped metal thing jutting up from the grass.

Grass, at least that *I recognize*, she thought, although she had never seen such vibrant and uniformly cut grass before.

As she looked toward the center of the city, the buildings got progressively higher until they reached a majestic tower situated right in the center. It appeared to still be under construction.

"I've never seen anything like this," she said to no one in particular

"I haven't either. At least, I don't think so . . ." Ryan said, his voice trailing off as conflicting memories from a past life came flooding back. "I think . . . I think it's something from a dream I had once." He walked as though in a trance through the grid of streets and cookie-cutter homes, each completely identical to the previous one.

Humanist, who was still leading the way, looked back at them, smiling. "We've worked hard building a society based on respect for our fellow man and scientific inquiry. It's enabled us to accomplish some amazing things—one of which is our modern medicine. Speaking of which, we'll be there soon and have you fixed up in no time!"

Ryan and Faith were struck by how out-of-place this city seemed. That's because the city was, in fact, from another place. The entire city was a transplant from Universe 42-A—not quite your world, although it was very similar to it. It had been cut from the fabric of that reality and placed in the Dying Lands very recently. None of the townspeople seemed to notice. They all seemed very happy and quite busy.

Some people peeked out of their doors and windows at the strange visitors. Others were busy at work in their yards and gardens, or washing shiny, hulking four-wheeled machines that were parked in front of their homes. Most smiled and gave a friendly wave from behind white picket fences. It was alien to Faith, but attractive. Peaceful. Like a place she would love to live. All memories of the Dying Lands seemed to fade the further they walked in the glowing artificial light of the city.

This place is nice. Really nice, she thought. She started to imagine owning a home of her own, raising beautiful green-eyed, red-headed children, having nice clothes, waiting for her loving man to return from work. As she took in the sights, her daydream turned to a gnawing in her stomach. Something seemed off about the city. She couldn't figure out what it was.

"We have wonderful lives here," said Humanist. "I live just down the street there on a corner lot," he added, motioning to a cookie-cutter home one block over with a well-manicured lawn and a swooping red wheel-machine parked in front. "The neighbors are great, too. We help each other out! And the thing is, we do it without the Book. You don't need all that stuff to know what a moral life looks like. We've evolved beyond the need for that, haven't we?"

Faith looked at Ryan. He seemed to be pondering, because something about Humanist's words rang true to him. He started to say something, but instead let out a quiet "huh."

They soon realized the city of Urbia was a circle, with different districts shaped like concentric rings, like a bullseye. They had just walked through the outer ring and were stepping into the next ring.

"This is the industrial zone," said Humanist. "This is where most of us work."

The buildings were a little taller now. There were more people. They all wore pristine-looking one-piece uniforms. Some rode strange two-wheeled machines. The buildings were made of glass and metal.

Faith watched in awe as massive wheel-machines pulled up to bigger and bigger buildings. Everyone seemed to have a place to go. They moved with purpose.

Suddenly, the pain in Faith's feet shook her out of her gawking stupor. "Owwww . . ." Her whole body hurt. She and Ryan with their tattered clothing, matted hair, and bloody wounds must have been quite a sight to the pristine citizens of Urbia. Ryan could feel it too. He stopped for a moment and took a knee. "I don't think I can go on another step."

"I'm so sorry. Of course, you need rest. Let's take the rest of our journey in style," said Humanist. He pulled a strange glowing device from his pocket, like a glass book with no pages, and pressed a few buttons on its surface. Within moments, a gleaming silver wheel-machine pulled up beside them. Humanist swung open its rear door and motioned inside. "Get in and take a seat. There's no reason for you poor folks to keep walking."

Faith gratefully slid into the rear seat beside Ryan and leaned up against him. He seemed lost in thought. He didn't look over as she put her hand on his arm.

Soon they crossed out of the sterile industrial zone and entered a place brimming with vibrant flashes of neon light. "This is the Pleasure District," said Humanist. "We offer everything you could possibly want! We have the best food, the best shows, the best music, everything! As hard as we work, and as short as our lives are, we make sure to fill it with wonderful sensual experiences! Life is short! Live a little!"

Ryan finally broke his silence. "Do you have bread and cheese here?"

Humanist beamed. "Do we have bread and cheese? You bet we do! Oh man, wait till you try this place!" He pressed a few buttons on his glass book and the machine came to a stop next to a bustling cafe with tables out front, filled with happy customers munching on bread and cheese and drinking beer. "This place has the best stuff you've ever tasted. They combined the bread and the cheese into one food. Brilliant! We call it Cheesy Bread!"

The three shuffled out of the vehicle and sat down at a nearby table. Faith looked around. People everywhere were laughing and dancing. Instead of the sterile jumpsuits of the industrial district, they wore garish multicolored designer clothing. Many wore makeup or colored wigs. Flashing neon signs blinked purple, red, green, blue, and orange, more pure and vibrant than anything Faith had seen in the Dying Lands, which now almost seemed a distant memory. She had already forgotten about the sunsets.

But something still felt off. She couldn't place it. That gnawing feeling in her stomach was still there. Next door to the Cheesy Bread Cafe was a purple sign that read "PLEASURE PALACE-BEAUTIFUL WOMEN-XXX-LIVE SHOWS." Faith looked away in embarrassment.

"We have destigmatized sex work in our city," said Humanist. "Our women here are treated with the utmost respect, with full agency and autonomy over what they do with their bodies. It's a wonderful thing that brings joy to many people in these dying lands! Don't be embarrassed! It's all about freedom here! We don't believe in giving up our freedoms to the words of some old Book."

Faith looked over at Ryan, who was still silent.

Within minutes, their table was filled with baskets of steaming bread—buttery, crispy, soft, and of course covered with melty cheese. A cute waitress in a green dress and roller skates brought out pitchers of ale.

If they'd still retained some sense of wariness in this place, the food made them forget themselves entirely. Faith and Ryan dove into the piles of bread with reckless abandon. It was the most delightful thing they had ever eaten. When they had sated their desperate hunger, they relaxed and ate more slowly as additional baskets were brought out. Each basket had a different variety of bread and cheese. Each combination had a unique twist that surprised and delighted. For both of them, the Dying Lands were feeling like a distant memory.

Then, suddenly, Faith was brutally jarred back to reality. Her eye caught a familiar man as he stumbled out of the Pleasure Palace—someone who caused all her memories of the Dying Lands to come rushing back, someone she knew. Their eyes met.

It was none other than Pastor. The one who had lit a fire in them and encouraged them to leave the comfort of Evangelion. He stood there dressed in the same garish designer clothing of the Pleasure District, and he had a beautiful woman on each arm.

Pastor froze, a look of embarrassment on his face. He then recovered, gave Faith a little smile, then turned and walked away. He said something to his female companions that made them giggle, and the three of them disappeared around the corner.

Ryan had seen it too, but his face didn't share the same horror that Faith knew was all over her face. He looked curious. Still deep in thought.

Humanist paid the tab and they all got back in the wheel-machine, which roared back to life, resuming its journey toward the center of the city. The gleaming tower, still under construction, loomed closer and closer.

They drove through several more districts on their way to the central tower. The maintenance district was filled with scruffy, dirty-looking working-class folks. They all wore strange glowing collars. In the financial district they saw rows and rows of office workers in glass skyscrapers furiously clacking away at strange-looking button boards with glowing pictures in front of them. In the political district, they saw no people at all: only beautiful mansions, imposing concrete buildings, and statues and monuments everywhere. The monuments depicted proud, chiseled faces and strong shoulders looking to the horizon. Bronze placards told stories of strength and conquest, discovery and invention.

Soon, they arrived at the center.

The tower was even more awe-inspiring up close. It was spiral-shaped, like an ancient Sumerian ziggurat, so high that its top was concealed by the clouds. Above, Faith and Ryan saw formations of small unmanned flying contraptions hovering to and fro, building the tower brick by brick with spinning rotors and clicking robotic arms. The tower was made of a different material than the other clean angular buildings of glass and steel. This tower was made of brown, rough-hewn stone.

"We have completely automated our building process so our citizens will enjoy more leisure time," said Humanist. "Our automatic, intelligent flying machines are a wonderful invention. You'll soon see them up close!"

Humanist opened the door for them and helped the two feeble pilgrims onto the street. "To access the resources and benefits of Urbia, you first need to meet our leaders and agree to their terms and conditions," he said. His cheery demeanor became more serious. "Help and healing is coming, I assure you. You will even be given a home of your own to settle down in if you like. Think of that—we could be neighbors! Our city's leaders await us on the top floor of this tower. Follow me."

Ryan finally broke his long silence.

"Faith . . . what if . . . what if this is where our journey has led us? Look at this place! Look at these people! There's not a Book in sight! No one here follows the King, if He even exists!"

They entered a cavernous front entrance to the tower. Their steps echoed on the stone floor. Workers and city officials turned and looked at the strange travelers. Ryan kept talking.

"If He does exist, He seems much more interested in watching His followers suffer than blessing their lives! Maybe the Golden City the Book speaks of was just a metaphor. Maybe we really do need to make our own Golden City here in the Dying Lands. Maybe we are the King we've been looking for."

The three of them stepped onto some sort of lift enclosed by glass. "This will take us to the top," said Humanist as he took out his glass book again. The door slid closed with a *whoosh.* The elevator began to move.

Faith suddenly realized what was wrong with Urbia. That gnawing feeling in the pit of her stomach twisted and lurched. Her heart began to pound. She grabbed Ryan's arm once again, the way she had always done from day one of their journey, gently nudging him, reminding him, keeping him on the path.

"Ryan, there are no children here."

"What?"

"There are no children here. I haven't seen a single child since we stepped foot in this city. Not one. Where are the kids? Where are the babies?"

Ryan was silent again. He shrugged, but a chill went up his spine. "Yeah . . . that's kind of weird."

They both looked at Humanist, who said nothing. He stared straight ahead, intently watching a little screen that counted the floors.

661 . . . 662 . . . 663 . . .

After a few more floors, the elevator shuddered to a stop.

The doors opened and they were met by a howling wind. They were on the roof of the tower in the open air. Drones whirred and hummed like bees, carrying material and fixing it in place. Clouds stretched out as far as the eye could see. They were far above the valley and the Dying Lands where there were no shadows, and the sun shone brightly and warmly. There was no Golden City to be seen.

"Welcome to the Tower of Urbia, the glory of man!" said Humanist, stretching out his arms and smiling widely.

Faith looked Humanist squarely in the face. "Where are the children? Where are the babies?!"

Humanist's smile disappeared.

"I suppose now is a good time to tell you that I am the leader of Urbia," he said flatly. "And you are in the Golden City. This is it. Your search has come to an end. I'm sorry if this feels disappointing to you, but it's time for you to open your eyes. You can have a good life here.

A prosperous one. You can do so much good for yourself and others! We can heal your wounds! You can work, play, and eat Cheesy Bread!"

"But this land is a dying one," said Faith. "None of us have much time left."

"This city is not a part of your land," said Humanist. "We were placed here, transplanted from another universe, just for you! And you can come back to our universe with us as these lands crumble and die, and all the lies and false legends die with them! We are your hope! We are your future! Repeat after me. 'Urbia is my hope. Urbia is my future. We will be happy here.'"

Ryan began to sway back and forth, as if he was being hypnotized. "Urbia is my hope. Urbia is my future. I will be happy here . . ."

"Ryan!" Faith snapped. Ryan blinked and came to his senses. He looked down at his cuts and bruises. He suddenly remembered himself.

"Humanist, where are all the kids?"

Humanist's facial expression went blank—as if the soul behind his eyes had disappeared. His eyes went black. "These are my terms and conditions."

Suddenly Ryan heard a baby crying. He whirled around to see a flying drone, carrying an infant child in its cold, robotic arms. It flew up to Humanist and placed the baby in his hands.

"To maintain peace, freedom, and prosperity in Urbia, only the babies I choose shall be allowed to live to adulthood. Our city can only feed so many. With too many people, our ability to maintain our harmonious world would collapse. Only the genetically pure, the intelligent, the team players, are chosen from among our offspring. The rest of them are dispatched here in this tower. They fuel our city. They fuel our machines. They give us this beautiful life. They are a gift, and they give their lives so that millions can experience peace. Other societies maintain peace through war and bloodshed. We do it simply by eliminating unthinking, unfeeling infants who feel no loss. It's a small price to pay!"

Ryan and Faith recoiled in horror as a circular door in the center of the floor opened, revealing a yawning pit of roaring flame. Searing heat leapt from the abyss and scorched their faces and hands. Above the roar of the fire, from deep below, they heard the sound of machinery, the whine of electricity generators, and drums. Drums beating a frenzied rhythm, like an ancient pagan ceremony attended by a thousand demons.

"These are the terms. Throw this clump of flesh and blood into the fire, power this city, and show you are ready to be one of us."

The flames licked out of the pit, threatening to light their tattered clothes like candle wicks. The sound of the furnace grew louder. The drums beat faster.

"You have to be kidding, right?" cried Ryan. "This is a joke, right? Some kind of a test? Who could do something so horrible?"

"Someone with a logical, rational mind," replied Humanist calmly. "If brought to the Dying Lands, this baby will suffer and die like everyone else who lives in that realm. If left here, the system collapses and we all die. Do you really want to doom the millions of people in this city because of your fragile sensibilities, or some lofty moral sense you got from an ancient Book? Are you really prepared to say that the millions of people who live in this city, all of whom sacrificed a human infant to live here, are wrong too? We need to enable human thriving for the greatest amount of people possible, and this is how we do it! Your Golden City awaits! A home, a rewarding career! You can settle down with each other and build a life together! And the Cheesy Bread! Don't forget about the Cheesy Bread!"

"What's our other choice?" asked Ryan.

Faith felt rage rising steadily within her. She couldn't believe Ryan was still engaging this man in conversation. Humanist replied flatly, "The other choice is we drag you out of the city and give you back to the Hollow Ones. This really shouldn't be hard. This baby was willingly donated by its parents for our survival and the continued success of the city. There is no loss here. No one will miss it. No one will feel pain. One act, and you get a life of peace and plenty!"

"'Before I formed you in the womb, I knew you . . .'" Faith was quoting from the Book. "'You shall not murder.'"

"Still quoting the stupid Book?" Humanist's face lost its dark emptiness and twisted into red rage.

Faith stood up straight. Her face was serene. She looked at Ryan with a gentle smile and then back at Humanist. "The Book is real. The King is real. We travel on His road, and we reject your terms and conditions. We will keep moving forward." She drew her humble sword from its sheath and held it up. "Do your worst."

Humanist sneered. "Very well."

And then he pushed Faith into the flames.

Her sword clattered to the ground as her body fell out of sight. Ryan tried to scream her name, but nothing came out. The fire roared brighter and higher as he leapt toward the roiling abyss, even though part of him already knew it was too late. The fire blackened his clothing as he reached the edge just in time to see Faith's body, already consumed, falling down into the depths of the void. There were no screams, no cries of agony. Only the sound of beating drums, whining generators, and her last words echoing in his head. And then Ryan's scream escaped.

Sorrow, rage, and guilt consumed him. He felt dizzy, sick to his stomach. He had no time to process it, since Humanist was walking toward him. Ryan grabbed Faith's sword, ran to the edge of the tower, and leapt off.

With thousands of flying machines in the air around the tower, he had a good chance of grabbing hold of one. He only had a split second. He reached out for the first drone, but it slipped out of his hands, sending him tumbling downward. He landed hard on a second drone and went careening the other way. Then he saw one heading straight for him, its robotic arms extended. By some miracle, his free hand found it and gripped tightly. With his last ounce of strength, he pulled himself up and onto the back of the machine. Glancing back, he saw Humanist, still holding the tiny baby in his arm.[50]

Ryan wrestled with the drone, his weight dragging it down as it flew along, trying to pull him back toward the tower. But he was too heavy, and kicking his legs this way and that, he was able to steer it toward the north end of the city. Against its cold, mechanical will, the flying machine took Ryan past the Political District, the Pleasure District, and finally to the Suburbs, slowly losing altitude all the way. It arrived at the edge of the city and dumped him on the ground in the darkness of the valley. It stared at him quizzically, then seemed to forget about him entirely, turning abruptly and flying back for its next task.

Ryan turned away, looking at the last leg of his journey. Ahead of him stretched a barren, windswept desert. Sands blew in the wind, obscuring everything ahead. There was no Golden City in sight. Ryan clutched Faith's sword, and his knees buckled beneath him.

---

[50] I know what you're thinking: what about the baby?! I wish I could tell you Ryan dug deep, found the hero within him, and saved the baby. I wish I could tell you the King Himself appeared and unleashed His holy wrath upon those who would kill babies for the sake of convenience. But I can't. The world is a brutal place, and evil is real. Children die, evil people kill them, and complacent people let them. Existence is full of suffering. Why does the King allow it? I don't know. Like I said, there are some books in the Archives I'm not allowed to open.

CHAPTER 17:

TUMBLEWEEDS AND TEMPTATION (AND ALSO A DRAGON)

Time takes it all, whether you want it to or not. Time takes it all, time bears it away, and in the end there is only darkness. Sometimes we find others in that darkness, and sometimes we lose them there again.

—Stephen King, *The Green Mile*

I resist the devil, and often it is with a fart that I chase him away.

—Martin Luther

Ryan staggered into the desert. The cracked ground stretched out before him in an endless patchwork of dry and dismal death. His tears fell wet and hot, but he had no time to grieve. He had to move on.

He moved as fast as his ragged, beaten body would allow him to, taking just one more desperate step every time he thought he could move no further. His mind raced with the advice he'd had pounded into his head time and time again on this bizarre dream/vision-quest thing: just keep moving forward. Reminding himself to just put one foot in front of the other could strangely be a powerful motivator even when the rest of him just didn't want to move at all.

Of course, having a roaming horde of zombies chasing you can be a powerful motivator as well. In fact, studies have shown that having a roaming horde of zombies chasing after you is the third most powerful motivator[51] for hiking through a desert wasteland where you'll almost certainly die of thirst if the Vulturaptors[52] don't get you first. And hoo boy, were there zombies chasing after him! The Hollow Ones outside the city gates had taken notice as the drone dropped him off on the northern end of Urbia, and they closed in fast.

You may be wondering at this point where on earth the Road was. Ryan didn't know, and Ryan didn't care.[53] He was lurching along the sandy desert floor, stumbling in any direction so long as it was away from Urbia. Somewhere in the screaming chaos of his mind, Ryan had the wild idea to just keep his eyes on the Golden City, road or no road. He looked frantically up but could see no lights and no city, only sand whirling through the air. He hurried drunkenly in the direction he thought was north, zigzagging across the wasteland like an ant some mischievous child has dropped a stick in front of so he'll lose his way.

"Gotta . . . keep . . . moving . . ." Ryan gasped as he moved into the desert, which somehow got dryer and deader than it had seemed before with every step. Low piles of rocks like gravestones were the only exception to the wide, flat landscape of dried, cracked earth. Not even cactuses would grow in this land of gnarled rock and death. "Just one more step. Just one more step."

He began to cackle, his mind having reached its limit. The human brain can take an incredible amount of pressure. But even the strongest will has its limit. Even the toughest mind can crack. And, no offense, but Ryan did not have the toughest mind. "Just one more step, step,

---

[51] The other two are running from the laser-pincers wielded by the seventeen-dimensional beings in Universe #5,692,341 and running from your wife after telling her to calm down.

[52] Exactly what they sound like.

[53] In fact, the Road had mostly been buried in sand throughout Temptation Desert, so Ryan's instinct was, miraculously, a good one. Everyone knows when you can't find a Road, at least try to keep your eyes on your destination. That's in the Book too, you know, though Ryan didn't know that, as his Book was miles and miles away.

always one more steeeeeep," he began to sing, laughing. The laugh of a maniac. "My friends are dead, my friends are dead, but I've gotta keep mooooooving. Just oooone mooooore step!"

No one applauded as he concluded his maniacal song. He just trudged forward, one shaky step in front of the other, not really remembering why or where he was going.

After what could have been minutes or hours, he finally could go no further, zombies or no. He looked behind him. The low moan of the Hollow Ones had been swallowed by the silence of the desert and the whistling of the wind. Urbia had disappeared from sight entirely, and he was alone.

"Hahaha! What's next, a tumbleweed?" Ryan said deliriously, licking his cracked, dry lips.

Just then, a tumbleweed rolled drunkenly past him and out of sight.

"Gotta be kidding me."

Dawn broke the horizon and beat down without mercy. Ryan collapsed against a red boulder, seeking refuge in its thin sliver of a shadow.

Grief is a funny thing. It doesn't hit you all at once, but rather it comes in waves. Sometimes the ocean of grief slowly subsides like a waning tide, and sometimes it takes you whole and buries you in its watery depths. Ryan got hit by a tidal wave. The sobs came hard and heavy. Ryan convulsed on the coarse sand. He didn't know who he was anymore—Christian, Ryan, just the figment of someone's imagination, or an NPC[54] in a cruel Matrix-style computer simulation designed by some sadistic god—but he still couldn't shake the image of Faith, innocent and pure, falling into the flames. He remembered her words: "We just keep moving forward." And he hated her for it.

---

[54] This means "non-player character," a character controlled by a computer rather than a human in a video game. You know, in case you're a boomer and don't understand the kids' references these days.

For her words had summoned another face: Matthew Fleming, sixteen, dying of cancer because there's no God and no meaning and no love in the universe. Just maverick molecules dancing on the head of a pin to a cacophony of meaningless nothing. He watched it again and again like the replay of a bad soap opera you can't turn off.

"Why?" he whimpered as the strange dreamland sun crept higher into the sky, robbing him of his shade and heating the sand beneath his skin. "Why, why, why . . . it doesn't make sense. It isn't fair. No, no, no, not Matty, not Matty, not Faith. Not me. Why me? This is a dream. This is all a dream. This isn't real. My other life . . . it isn't real either. Nothing matters. Everything is a lie."

He shut his eyes tight as the sun baked his skin. *If only I could go back and live my life before Matt, before everything. I'd rather Matt never existed. I'd rather Faith never existed, if she ever existed at all.*

"What's happenin'?" A cold voice broke the hot silence of the desert.

Ryan scrambled to his feet and whirled around. There, sitting in a comfortable lounge chair, was the Devil. His suit was as smart as ever. He sipped an old-fashioned root beer float. A tall floor lamp stood next to him, along with a fine side table. He was reading a book. Ryan recognized the cover through the fog of his multidimensional memories: *Harry Potter and the Prisoner of Azkaban.*

"What are you doing here?" Ryan asked dumbly. It's always embarrassing to be caught crying when you think you're alone, even when it's by the Devil.

The Devil shrugged. "Doing some light reading."

He ignored Ryan and went back to his book. He chuckled. "Hermione is a spunky one."

"So . . . is Harry Potter satanic after all?" Ryan asked, wiping the dusty tears from his face. While, of course, the Devil is always bad news, at least he focused Ryan's energy and attention on something and got his thoughts off the things that would drive him to the brink of madness. An enemy can give you a reason to fight.

"What?" asked the Devil. "Oh, not at all. Even the Devil enjoys a good book from time to time."

He snapped his fingers and the book disappeared with a puff of smoke. A second chair appeared next to him. On the table appeared a tall, cool bottle of ice water labeled "Fiji."

"Come, sit. Drink," he said, gesturing apathetically. "Or don't. I don't really care one way or the other."

"You're trying to trick me," Ryan said, his anger rising. "Just like you did last time. You tried to kill me."

"I've tried to kill you, like, three or four times now," the Devil said. "The house of prosperity? That was me. The rockslide? Guilty as charged."

"You killed Faith!" Ryan shouted. He found his courage and marched forward, brandishing her sword.

The Devil didn't flinch. He just shrugged again. "No. Some things are decided by a Fate greater than I. I didn't have a say in that one. I would have made it more painful, if I'm being honest with you."

Ryan raised his—or rather, her—sword. The Devil raised his hands defensively. "Hey, hey, I'm just saying. I'm the Devil. It's what I do. Chill out, man."

Ryan swung, the sword aimed straight and true for the Devil's neck.

The Devil moved faster than wind, sound, and thought. One second, he was casually sitting in his lounge chair in the middle of the desert. The next, he was towering over Ryan, his eyes glowing in menace and hate. He grabbed the sword and hurled it high into the air. It landed some twenty yards away, clattering on some broken boulder out of Ryan's sight.

"I. Said. SIT," he growled. His hand, larger, claw-like somehow, grabbed Ryan by the chest and shoved him violently into the seat next to him. Then, just like that, he dusted himself off and sat back down, returning to his former diminutive state. He looked around, not even appearing to notice Ryan. "I really wish you'd drink that water," he said casually.

"No," Ryan grunted.

The Devil shrugged. "It's not magic or anything. I just thought you might be thirsty."

Ryan sat for a few moments. His tongue darted out and licked his chapped lips. The water did look good. He tried not to think about it, which only made him think about it more. If you ever want to get good and thirsty, try *not* thinking about drinking water. Especially when the Devil is sitting in front of you with a tall, cool bottle of Fiji water. And, you know, the whole dying-of-thirst-in-the-middle-of-the-desert thing.

I could draw this out and explain to you how the sun continued to beat down and the Devil continued to stare at Ryan as every new bead of sweat dropped down from his forehead. Minutes on end went by, and the Devil didn't say a word. It was very awkward.

But nobody likes awkward,[55] so I'll skip ahead a bit: Ryan eventually gave in and drank the water. He drank every last drop. He drank so much that his aching belly threw it all up, and he vomited right onto the Devil's shiny shoes. The Devil summoned a towel and another bottle of water—Dasani this time—and Ryan drank all that, too.

Hey, don't be too hard on Ryan here: the spirit is willing, but the flesh is pretty dang thirsty.

His immediate problem of thirst solved, Ryan turned his attention to the more pressing matter: that the Devil was sitting right in front of him, tempting him in an eternal battle for the fate of the world and maybe even his soul.

---

[55] I can't even bring myself to watch that episode of *The Office* where Michael promised those kids college tuition. As you humans say, so much cringe. And I don't even have a face with face muscles that can cringe.

"So did I just sell my soul for a bottle of water? Is that what that was?" Ryan said, settling into his chair.

The Devil shrugged. "No. I told you it wasn't magic or anything.[56] I just thought you looked thirsty. How am I supposed to tempt you if you're an emaciated corpse?"

Ryan smiled. "Ah, so you *are* trying to tempt me? Guess you let that one slip."

The Devil laughed pleasantly. "That's no secret. I *am* the Devil after all. It's kinda my job."

As usual, the Devil made Ryan continue the conversation. Ryan was really starting to hate that about him.

"Aren't I supposed to fight you, like you turn into a dragon, and I go get my sword? I use a mighty sword and a stalwart shield and fend off your fiery darts?"

"Eh, that's kinda old-school. I figured we'd just do a battle of the wits. They're more in vogue these days."

"So, what's the offer?"

"Same as always. Give up. Abandon your quest. Go home. There's nothing left for you here."

"And what do you get out of it?"

"You don't ring the bell. You don't wake the King. The Dying Lands are covered in fire and death. I win, kiddo."

Something happened in Ryan's heart at that moment. He opened his mouth to refuse the Devil, but no words came out. He shut it again. He'd thought it would be easy to turn him down, as he was so obviously tempting him with evil. But discussing things with the Devil is almost always a bad idea, and the Devil's words have a way of worming their way into one's heart. Sometimes those who laugh at the Devil find that he has the last laugh after all.

---

[56] Don't worry. The Devil was actually telling the truth here. He does that more often than you'd think. You know, for being Satan and all.

"Say the words, kid," the Devil said softly now. "Say the words and you're out of here. No tricks this time. No faulty magic spell that sends you careening through space and time. That would have been fun, though, watching your body get torn limb from limb or get crushed in a black hole. This time, I'll settle for you leaving this place and never coming back. You've got heart, Ryan. You made it further than anyone ever has. But you're never going to make it across this desert. What do you say we wake you up and send you back where you belong?"

Whether it was the water or some power of Hell or just Ryan's delirious, beaten body, he suddenly wanted nothing more than just to go home. The Devil was right. Like it or not, the Devil was right. There was nothing left for him here. Faith was dead. Faith, the only pure thing in this world—maybe the only pure thing in *any* world—was dead for no reason at all. His one friend in this messed-up dream had been killed, because of course she had.

The Devil was still alive. The Hollow Ones were still roaming the lands, consuming everything like a great insatiable machine. Evil men like the Smiling Preacher and Health-and-Wealth and those apathetic followers of the King in Evangelion were doing just fine. But Faith, the one sacred thing in this world, the one good, undefiled thing in all the Dying Lands, had died. If that wasn't evidence that there was no King, no God—or that if He did exist, He was a real jerk—he didn't know what was.

"Let me show you something, Ryan," the Devil said. He didn't wait for a response. Suddenly, they were no longer in the desert. In the blink of an eye, they were sitting in their chairs in a hospital room where a sixteen-year-old boy was dying of cancer.

"No," Ryan whispered. Now, the Dying Lands were as a dream, and the Earth he'd grown up in was bitterly and painfully real. The sterile hospital smell humans hate so much stung his nostrils.

Ryan felt a hand on his shoulder. It was the Devil. "I'm sorry, Ryan," he said. It sounded like he meant it, too.

Beep. Beep. Beep. The machine attached to the boy punctuated the silence with a cold, hard reminder of just how mortal humans really are. *Beep. Beep. Beep.* Ryan winced with each piercing tone. Every life was ultimately just that pulsing beep underneath it all, and every life would one day return to silence. Some far too soon.

"I can take you back," the Devil said after a few moments.

"Why would I ever want to come back here?" Ryan said, the sting of tears in his eyes.

"You misunderstand," the Devil said. He folded his hands. "I can take you back—to before any of this ever happened. That lump in little Matty's brain? I can take it out. I've gotten permission from the guy upstairs. He lets me do things sometimes."

Ryan was hot with anger. "So just like that, he's back? You snap your—your devil fingers and everything's the way it was supposed to be?"

"Just like that," the Devil said, smiling his hollow smile.

"What's the catch? And don't tell me there's not a catch because I've started to figure out how these deals with devils work."

"I'm going to be honest with you," the Devil said. "There is, of course, a catch." He adjusted his tie, and Ryan's head lurched back into his seat. His eyes rolled back into his head. And he saw a vision of what could be, if he would just say yes.

He saw himself playing *Halo* on his Xbox—a very real memory from his other life. He remembered this day vividly. He wanted to shut his eyes, to make it all go away, but, of course, his eyes were already shut. He had to watch this scene play out, like that guy in *A Clockwork Orange*.

He watched himself as his phone rang—the phone call that changed his life forever, the phone call when he learned Matty had cancer. "Hey, Mom. What's up?" he heard himself saying. "Yeah? I told you it was nothing to worry about. Haha. Yeah. Well, that's a relief. Fish tacos? Yeah. Where at? Alberto's? I'll be there."

He blinked, and the scene changed. Matty playing disc golf with him at the world-famous Huntington Beach course. The two of them surfing before he had to drop off his kid brother at high school. Scenes of them experiencing all the life that was taken away far too soon.

But something was missing. He couldn't place his finger on just what that was at first, but eventually, as the scenes flashed in his mind—Matty going to prom, Matty getting married, Matty being the best man at his wedding—it came to him: he never saw Matt reading his Bible. He never saw Matty insisting the rest of the family pray before dinner. He never saw Matt, tears in his eyes, begging Ryan to go to church with him. Matty was alive, but he didn't have his faith.

Ryan snapped back from the vision, and there he was, sitting on a leather chair in the middle of the desert with the Devil, and it was all but a dream again.

"So, whaddya say, kid? Just say the word, and it's all yours."

Ryan looked down. His fingers were clenched white hot on his knees. He dug his nails into his skin, the weight of the moment stressing him to a breaking point.

Ryan thought, long and hard. Save Matt, and go back. Or leave his brother, dead and cold and rotting beneath some slab of granite with a feel-good, kitschy saying on it in a mowed lawn in Covina somewhere. And go forward.

He took a deep breath and looked at the Devil.

The Devil smiled, a glimmer of hope in his eyes. "Will you take the deal?"

Ryan opened his mouth and said, "Yes."

Or rather, he *almost* said yes. And what a disaster that would have been! If you've read this far, you've probably gathered that making deals with the Devil is *not* a good idea.

Through some twist of fate or luck, as Ryan opened his mouth to say yes, abandon his quest, doom the Dying Lands, and hand the Devil a major victory, his hands clenching tight on his thighs felt something in his pocket. He idly slipped his hand into his pocket and found a humble, crumpled-up piece of paper. He didn't pull it out and read it. He didn't need to. In that moment, he remembered what it said. The words weren't just written on the scroll—they were Matthew's words. In a flash, he was back in the hospital room, as his brother looked up at him with eyes full of faith: "*Walk forward*."

With great effort, through gritted teeth, Ryan cursed the Devil. He defied the darkness. He looked him in the eye and said, "No."

Now, I don't know everything there is to know about the Devil, but I do know he *hates* being told no.

The Devil's smile froze on his face. "What?"

"I said no," Ryan said, clenching his fist with ever-increasing resolve. "If . . . even if you're telling the truth, and you *could* bring Matty back . . . that wasn't him. He didn't . . . he didn't have his faith. I'm starting to see it all so clearly. Maybe I'll regret this—I already kind of do—but I don't want Matty on those terms. That's not him. Matty without his faith isn't Matty."

Ryan winced as he said the words, already wishing he could take them back, tell the Devil yes, and have his brother again. "But I can't change the past. I can't go back. I have to go forward."

"Suit yourself," said the Devil.

"You're . . . you're not mad?" asked Ryan.

"Nah. No biggie," he responded.

Ryan got up and brushed himself off. He turned toward the Golden City in the distance, which was now shining brightly through the calming sandstorm. "Well, I guess I better keep moving."

"Yeah, now *that* is gonna be an issue," said the Devil.

Ryan froze and turned toward the Devil. His bald head protruding from his freshly pressed suit started to turn a green hue. His eyes were now slitted yellow. He slowly grew larger and larger. Wings ripped out of the back of his suit coat. Within moments, Ryan no longer faced a thin, creepy white guy sitting in a chair. He faced an enormous Dragon.

Before he had time to react, the Dragon struck out with its claws, opening a gash in Ryan's chest. He fell backward and cried out in pain. He scrambled to his feet and backpedaled away from the hulking mass of scales, wings, and fire in front of him. Fire? Yes, fire. The Dragon was breathing fire, as all good dragons do, scorching the earth this way and that in an attempt to snuff out Ryan's life. Ryan dove behind one of the leather chairs just in time as a fiery blast came his way. The Dragon continued to grow larger and larger, blotting out the sun with darkness as it relentlessly came on.

Ryan ran, jumping from boulder to boulder, narrowly avoiding blast after blast of fire and death. With each of the Dragon's mighty roars he could feel the heat of the flames licking at his back, and he could smell his own burning flesh.

"I liked the 'battle of wits' part better," he muttered between gasping breaths. He looked to his left and saw a welcome sight: the sword the Devil had cast aside. If he could just make one last desperate dash, maybe he could get it and stand a chance. More likely, he'd die, but at least it would be an epic death. And now it seemed right: the Devil had been there all along, a thorn in his side for the whole journey. A holy hatred flamed within him. He couldn't beat the Devil, but he wanted him to pay. Ryan steeled himself, took a breath, and waited. When the Dragon finished yet another scorching blast, he leaped, running for the sword. Now it was twenty feet away. Now ten. Now he was diving for it as another cyclone of fire ripped toward him.

He grasped the sword and turned. Without thought, without fear, he stood tall and charged toward the Dragon. Ryan Fleming, thirty-three, from the Valley, who'd gone to Foothill Elementary and San Fernando High and worked for an enterprise-level IT software firm, marched forward to face all the power of Satan and Hell in the form of a scaly Dragon with fire for breath and malice in his eyes.

And he got knocked flat on his back with one swoop of the Dragon's wings.

The Dragon laughed, if dragons can laugh. It came out more like a roar and was accompanied by more fire. Ryan rolled out of the way and stumbled to his feet. He looked down at his sword, and to his shock, it was glowing a frosty blue. And for a moment—just a moment—as he stared at his reflection on its steely surface, he saw fierce emerald eyes staring back at him, surrounded by strands of ember.

"Well, that's new," he muttered. He held it aloft, and for the first time, he saw what looked like fear in the Dragon's eyes. It growled and hissed—and most importantly, it hesitated. That moment was all Ryan needed. He ran in and closed the gap, and before the Dragon knew what hit him, a sword of pure frost had plunged into his heart. He screamed at the sky, one last blast of fire, and to any who were watching it would have looked as though a geyser of flames had shot to the heavens.

The Dragon collapsed, defeated, and Ryan was once again just a weary traveler, the sword was just an ordinary sword, and he was still lost in the middle of the desert. He looked around. No one was there to witness his act of heroism, his big battle with the Dragon in the middle of nowhere. He wondered how many feats of bravery in battles big and small, physical and spiritual, countless pilgrims had performed that would never be written of in books or sung about in songs.

He paused for a moment. Then, he walked on, heading toward the city of gold.

CHAPTER 18:

THE RIVER INFINITE

To go back is nothing but death; to go forward is fear of death, and life everlasting beyond it. I will yet go forward.

—John Bunyan, *The Pilgrim's Progress*

All those moments will be lost in time, like tears in rain. Time to die.

—Roy Batty, *Blade Runner*

Burned, blackened, bloodied, and bruised, Ryan stumbled across the desert. He had not found the Road (nor would he, as it was buried under twenty-three feet of sand some three miles to the northwest of him.) With no Book to guide him, no sword to protect him, and neither water nor food to sustain him, he could do nothing but walk on to whatever doom was in store for him.

There was a kind of peace in it. He fully expected to die, and that was OK. He had done his part. He had walked on. He had made it further than he ever expected to. The birds would peck at his corpse,[57] and the circle of life would continue, at least until the Dying Lands were completely destroyed in a few weeks' time. Against all odds, across the white sands, the tiny figure pressed on.

[57] Technically it would be the Vulturaptors, but mercifully, Ryan did not know about those.

At the far edge of the desert, a river of black flowed silently against a white shore. There were no sounds: no birds chirping, no wind whispering across the soft desert sands. The waters stretched out endlessly to the horizon. On the near shore, a desert that seemed to be without end. On the far shore, a city of gold.

Footsteps broke the unnatural quiet. Ryan, bloody, beaten, ragged, and tired, emerged from behind a sand dune and made his way to the waters. He stood in shock at the sheer size of the river. It swallowed everything in one's vision. It had a way of blocking all thought and threatened to swallow you up with its vastness.

"No boats to cross the river, I guess," Ryan said to no one in particular. He'd still not grown used to not having anyone to talk to, what with Faith being dead and all. "It probably doesn't matter that no pilgrims ever made it this far. They'd all probably drown anyway. And no wonder." He looked despairingly at the swift waves, silently billowing past him from right to left. There was no real way to cross other than plunging right in.

Ryan took a deep breath. "Sometimes, all we can do is go forward," he said. His voice sounded shaky and unsure. But he'd come this far. He'd lost Faith, and he'd all but forgotten his old world. He had nothing left to lose, and that's a dangerous kind of man. He took a step into the water.

"Gah!" he cried. It felt as though a thousand daggers of ice were stabbing his foot all at once.

He took a step back. He looked behind him. "There is nothing for you there," he reminded himself, though he still didn't sound so sure. "Go forward."

He put his foot in the river again. The cold was no less intense, but this time, he kept it firmly in the current. It sank to a mucky bottom. After a moment, he put his other foot in. One foot in front of the other. Then another step. Then another. One step at a time. It was freezing cold, and every inch of the way was misery, but he took another step just the same.

Sometimes, when you think you can go no further, you take one more step. And then, somehow, you take another. And that's what Ryan did. The ice chilled his bones. He looked back and was astonished to see he was a hundred feet from the shore he'd left minutes ago. He turned and despaired as he saw the Golden City seemed no closer. Still, he picked up his foot from the rocky bottom of the river, and he took another step.

Soon, the waters were up to his waist. He was numb where the water was touching him, and he was chilled from the whipping wind where it wasn't. Misery, misery, misery all around! Every square inch of him was miserable. He thought of the warm hearths of Urbia, of the comfort of Evangelion, of his little cottage in the City of Destruction. Oh, what he wouldn't have given to go back!

But he pushed these thoughts from his mind and tried to replace them with another thought. With great effort, he imagined a homely room of silver and a bed of soft velvet in a city made of gold. He'd dine in that city tonight and sleep like a god.

"*It's not real, you know*," he heard a voice whisper. The Devil. He looked around, but neither the man in the suit nor the dragon were anywhere to be seen. The sound seemed to come from within him, from around him, from the water itself. "*The city. It's made-up. It's a lie. Turn around. Go back. Learn to love the Dying Lands.*"

"You're a liar," Ryan responded, his voice wavering with the cold. "You've always been a liar. Go away!"

Silence responded to him, and now he was sure he was going insane.

"Must go forward," he said through chattering teeth. The water was up to his chest now. The City might have been a little closer, but he might have been imagining it.

He pressed on for what felt like hours. He noticed the Golden City, with its white banners blowing in the breeze and its Belltower stretching impossibly toward the heavens, had shifted to his right. Or rather, he had shifted to the left, the mighty current pulling him as he trudged on through the icy blackness. He looked back again and saw the Dying Lands had begun to fade behind him. The city looked more and more real as he took each step, and the Dying Lands looked more and more like the dream.

Between him and the Golden City, Ryan saw a rock formation slowly growing larger. He adjusted his course, being much in need of a rest. After a few minutes, he pulled himself up on the slick grey rock, covered in moss and mist. He estimated himself to be about halfway through the river, though units of time and distance started to seem fuzzy to him the further he got out in the water. All he knew was that he was on a lonely rock in an infinite river, somewhere between Heaven and Hell. Ryan beat his chest for warmth, something he had seen in a movie once, though he was having trouble remembering what exactly a movie was. It didn't help, anyway.

Now that some feeling was returning to his lower half, sharp pains previously hidden by numbness electrified his nerves. He was freezing to death, quite literally. Thunder boomed somewhere above him. A soft rain began to fall. It soon turned into a pounding hail.

"This is just miserable!" he cried to no one at all. Silence swallowed his words. "Hey, King!" No response. Not even an echo. "King Guy who supposedly exists! If You're there, answer me!"

He turned toward the Golden City. It did not respond. "Why have You forsaken me?!" he screamed, an echo of something he'd heard a universe and a lifetime ago. The only response was the pounding of the ice.

Some all-powerful King, he thought. Or was someone whispering that into his ear? He couldn't tell. The voice of doubt came from within him, it came from around him. It might have been the Devil. It probably didn't matter where it came from. It only mattered that it was there, causing the poison of doubt to seep into his mind.

He slipped back into the water, praying the numbness would return, and fast.

The waters rose as he pressed on. Now it was up to his chest, now his neck. A thick fog clouded his mind, and then, a thick fog rolled in over the river, obscuring his vision of the Golden City. The waters rippled from the assault of ice from the sky. After a few minutes that stretched on like hours and days—did time have any meaning anymore?—he wasn't even sure he was going in the right direction. His feet groped for any kind of foothold in the slippery muck at the bottom of the river.

"*You're not going to make it*," he heard a voice say. He didn't bother looking around this time. "*You're not enough*."

Just then, his foot reached for another foothold and found only a gaping void beneath him. He spluttered and flailed about as he realized he could no longer touch the bottom. The waters were whipping about him. The chop was getting stronger here, and the Golden City was fast passing him by on the distant shore.

A wave pushed him under, and he was shocked beneath the surface of the water to see a face. A cold, dead, ghastly face rose up in front of him and began to speak.

It was Radical from the City of Destruction. "You're a fool," Radical said, laughing at him. "All that 'Golden City' stuff was fun when we were young and naïve. I can't believe you didn't grow out of that phase. And now, look at you: dying in a cold river in the wilderness all alone. All for nothing!" Radical threw his head back and laughed.

Ryan turned away and desperately flailed for the surface.

But he only saw another face.

Health-and-Wealth spoke: "You could have had riches, you know. Wealth unfathomable!"

He turned but only saw another ghost. Pastor did not speak but looked away sadly. He saw the Mayor of the City of Destruction pointing and laughing, Mr. Neckbeard lecturing him on all the reasons the King does not exist. And he saw Faith, murdered and burned and dead and gone—yet another person he failed to protect. The visions came faster now: himself in another life at a computer looking at shameful images late at night, looking for solace at the bottom of a bottle, suffering another meaningless night in his lonely apartment in a city full of people he did not know, care about, or love. An evil man atop a wretched tower, holding an innocent child he'd failed to save. Failure after shameful failure, defeat after resounding defeat, no matter which way he turned, all echoing with the whisper that he was a nobody who lived on an insignificant blue speck careening through uncaring space. Face after face of people he had let down and betrayed in both his lives swam toward him in an unending parade of his own failures.

Their accusing, jeering voices melted into one dissonant chorus singing as one: "You're not enough. You're not enough." His funeral dirge. And the worst part was that Ryan knew they were right. He wasn't enough. He had failed.

Ryan gave up. His body sank like a stone into the dark depths. He fell deeper and deeper beneath the waves, a black silhouette against a vortex of ghosts, a void of silence against a chorus of laughter. He frantically loosened his belt and dropped his sword. He struggled to pull off the rest of his clothes and gear, casting them into the infinite depths. But still he sank.

Blackness took his naked form. The swirling ghosts faded from electric blue to a distant brown. He was dying. He breathed in, and the icy water filled his lungs.

As he died, he dreamt he felt a warm, soft hand take his own, and he knew no more.

CHAPTER 19:

THE GOLDEN CITY

Is everything sad going to come untrue?

—Samwise Gamgee, *The Return of the King*

There are two ways to describe a sunrise, and neither is sufficient. First, there is the mechanical, technically accurate approach. You can tell a child a sunrise is just when the sun comes up in the morning—or more accurately, when the earth rotates so that the sun is in view again. You can tell him that a sunrise is actually an illusion, and that his brain is just translating the phenomenon of sunlight passing through the atmosphere as "beautiful" when really it is the most ordinary thing in the world.

The second way to describe a sunrise is to write volumes and volumes attempting to capture its beauty and its true and deeper meaning. You can write poems, songs, plays, epics, symphonies, and entire libraries of majestic prose in an attempt to chase the meaning of a sunrise. After thousands of years of study, I've decided this approach is the better one in the end. A sunrise is nothing more or less than the sun rising. It is a dawn. A new start. A new beginning. The best authors and poets know they cannot describe a sunrise, and so they admit defeat and just call it a brilliant dawn or a new morning or a beautiful sight and leave it at that.

So it is with trying to describe the Golden City. I could tell you it is a city of gold, and that would be the truest thing in the world while paradoxically being the most insufficient, gross, and vulgar way to describe the place. In many ways, it's just called the Golden City because that's the best way to communicate it to three-dimensional creatures stuck in the suffocating limits of time and space. Nonetheless, to human eyes, it appears as a breathtaking city of gold.

And this is what Christian's eyes saw as he sputtered up water on the silver shore. Though dark mists had surrounded him as he crossed the River Infinite, now he beheld a swift sunrise that never ended, sands of the purest, most sparkling white, and a city of gold that seemed to stretch on forever not far from the coast. He looked back, expecting to see the black river and the parched desert of the Dying Lands beyond, but they were not there. A grey shroud, as though a rain cloud blocked the world he had come to know as his own from view. It was as though a great curtain had been raised behind him, and already he began to forget. He looked down and saw that he was clothed in robes of the purest white and sandals of leather and gold.

He walked up to the Golden City and banged on the gates, made of gold and shot through with silver, gemstones, and pearls. They opened softly and he slipped inside.

Streets of gold stretched as far as his eye could see. Dwellings ranging from humble hovels to great, sprawling mansions dotted the alleyways and byways. While it was packed impossibly dense with buildings of all shapes and sizes, it also seemed to stretch on forever, seeming bigger and bigger the more you walked on.

What Christian did not expect was how busy and bustling the Golden City would be. It was, of course, a city, and a city means people. But every mention of the Golden City had simply summoned imagery of people quietly sitting around as though on clouds, playing harps or flutes and whispering to one another in hushed tones.[58]

This was quite different from the Reality in which he now found himself. It was loud, and joyfully so. A party, really. Great crowds broke out in spontaneous song and dance. Children played in the streets. Old men—were they old? Or were they young? It was suddenly hard for him to tell—smoked cigars and drank beer and debated theology and laughed and argued and laughed some more. A fat man who looked vaguely familiar sat on a rock of chalk and sketched a ladybug. Somewhere, a band played some indescribable genre of music that sounded like a mix of all genres of human music and some you people haven't even invented yet. All symphonies of all ages singing together for the King.

The smells of the Golden City I can only make a meager attempt at explaining to you: like morning coffee and the smell of your lover and freshly cut grass all in one—but a lot less disgusting than that sounds. Ugh. Your human language is just so limited and shallow when it comes to describing Real Things and Things That Matter. The food was to die for: carne asada, fish tacos, breakfast burritos, and, of course, the finest cheese you can only dream of in your world. Everyone did what they wanted and had everything in common. People worked hard, played hard, ate and drank hard, and slept with bellies as full as their hearts. There was no night, so people slept when they wanted to and woke when they felt like it and took afternoon naps whenever they pleased.[59]

Christian walked as if in a dream through the city streets, although this dream felt more real than his waking life. He might have explored for weeks or years or eternities within eternities. Even I can only guess

---

[58] He didn't know it, but he'd gotten this impression from *The Far Side*, a "comic book" from your human world. And all those old Donald Duck cartoons.
[59] Customer surveys indicate that limitless naptime is one of humans' favorite elements of the Golden City. The fish tacos also rank highly.

at how long he spent there. Besides, it would be fruitless. Time really has no meaning in the Golden City. He saw friends and enemies and acquaintances and those who would have been fast friends in his past life if he'd ever met them. He met people who had died long ago, people from other worlds, and people who had yet to die in his own world. He played cribbage and poker and euchre and chess and Go. He learned the banjo and the cello. At one point, weeks or years or who-cares-because-time-has-no-meaning into his stay, he had a nice, long conversation with a boy of sixteen, a boy with no cancer and no pain and no giant lump in his brain turning him into a vegetable.

All of this in one sigh of the wind, one brief, fleeting moment in an infinity of joy and pleasure.

At length, he came to the center of the city, if indeed eternity can have a center. He turned the corner one day and there it was: the Belltower of the King, stretching up into the heavens, the center of reality and the axis of eternity. At its peak, a bell of gold. At its base, a humble, wooden door. Christian knew it was time to enter. And he somehow knew that he would not look upon the Golden City again for a very, very long time.

Christian entered. The interior of the Belltower was cast with the same brilliant light as the rest of the city. A simple rope hung down from the top of the tower, stretching so high up that he could not see the top. Ryan pulled on the rope, and the bell rang out.

The Golden City melted away, as though it were all a dream and he were waking up. Or perhaps as though he were falling asleep again. Memories came flooding back to Christian—or was it Ryan?

Recollections of two lives lived in two very different worlds converged on him like the waters of the Red Sea crashing in on the armies of the Pharaoh. He blinked, and found he was no longer in the simple Belltower. He was now in a great study with windows that looked out over time and space. One wing of the hall contained shelves holding books without number.

A man with a grey beard sat at a desk and wrote quietly in a volume bound in red and laced with gold.

"Mr. King?" Christian asked. "Err—Your Majesty?"

The man stopped writing and closed the book. He stood and looked at Christian. He smiled at him. "You've arrived."

"Yes. I rang the bell," he said. "Are . . . are the Dying Lands saved?" As the bell rang, it had all come back to him: the struggles, the pain, the loss. Faith. Matt. Grief.

"Indeed. The Dying Lands are saved," the King said. "Have a look for yourself." He gestured toward a large window on the far side of the room. It seemed to look out at a sea of stars, infinitely vast. Ryan approached. He looked out the window and gazed through a spiral of universes, all realities dancing to the music of the spheres. All worlds revolving around and converging upon the room in which he stood face to face with the King.

The starfield faded, and the room seemed to soar like a spaceship over the Dying Lands. The City of Destruction was there, but it was whole again. There was neither fire nor brimstone careening toward it any longer. Homes stood proud and tall where craters had hollowed out the earth. Depression Swamp was now a flowering meadow surrounded by great oak trees. Happiness and joy covered the earth where sadness and sorrow had once reigned. Evangelion was still there, but its glass bubble was shattered, and its people filled the whole earth, doing the will of the King across all the Dying Lands. Most strikingly, a spring had broken through the earth and watered Temptation Desert, turning it into a sparkling sea. Translucent people turned whole again.

"It's—it's like time is working backward," Ryan said.

"Well, yes. And then again, no," the King replied. "Though that's a fine enough way of putting it. I created Time, and it bends to My will. We are more outside Time than anything."

"I don't understand," Ryan said. "Did I save the world?"

"Yes, you rang the bell, as you were destined to do," the King said.

"But . . . but I didn't make it," Ryan said, feeling a sense of shame. "I gave up. I didn't make it through the River. Someone pulled me out. I wasn't enough."

"That's right: you weren't enough," the King said. "You were never meant to be enough. You were only asked to be faithful. You were only asked to keep on going forward."

Ryan looked out again and saw a man with a burden on his back struggling along the King's Road, battling giants and fighting dragons and escaping dungeons. He saw an echo of this man, and then another, and then another, until they all blurred together. Thousands—maybe millions—of pilgrims converging through space and time to travel along the King's Road and reach the Golden City. Some made it. Most did not. Finally, like something out of one of your human movies, the image came lurching to a halt and focused in on two figures: a man and a woman struggling up a peak toward an old, rugged cross. Ryan recognized himself, and he remembered in full now.

"Where were You?" he whispered. "Why did I need to ring the bell to wake You up? Why were You sleeping? Did You ever care?"

"I was there," the King said quietly. "I was there with you all along. And I was also here, writing your story. You'll get to read it one day, you know. It will make more sense then. The meaning of the story is hard to discern for the person who is living it. But every detail is here. Your friends, your enemies. Health-and-Wealth, the Blackmuck. Pastor."

"What happened to Pastor, anyway?" Ryan asked, remembering.

The King smiled sadly. "Not all stories end in glory. His part was to help you along. Though there may be hope for him yet. But his story is not yours, and your story is now at an end. Though in another sense, it is just beginning."

There was a wrestling match inside the pilgrim: the memories of Christian and Ryan were locked in an epic struggle to the death. And Christian's were losing.

He struggled to remember. "My friend's name . . . was Faithful—no, wait. It was Faith," he said. But he could not remember her face.

"No . . . my brother. Matthew. Little Matthew. Why?" He became angry. Or rather, the anger, hurt, pain, and fear that had built up over the years bubbled to the surface. "Why did You let him die? Why did You kill him?"

"Does not the Author have power over those in the Book?" the King said.

"It's just not fair," Ryan said. The feeble statement seemed inadequate in the presence of the King. He knew he was treading on sacred ground, and he knew beyond doubt that questioning the King in this way could result in his death. But he pressed on anyway. He had to wrestle with the angel. He had climbed the ladder of Jacob and the stairway to Heaven, and he would be answered, death or no. "Why—why did Matthew die?"

The King looked at him, eye to eye. Ryan felt a terrible wrath and a mighty love all at once. "That is not the question, Ryan. The question is why did Matthew ever live? Why do good things happen at all? Chaos. Chaos and darkness. That is what your world once was. And hovering over the surface of the waters, I brought light. I brought goodness. I knew there would be struggles. I knew there would be pain. In fact, I'd already seen it. I'd already lived it."

He suddenly whisked himself across the room with a stunning and terrible speed and embraced Ryan. Tears fell from His eyes. "I cannot tell you why, Ryan. No one is allowed to learn the why. They could not handle mysteries so bright."

He drew back, holding Ryan by the shoulders. His eyes were wet with tears. "I cried every tear with you, Ryan. I felt every stab of pain, every doubt. I heard every scream into your pillow. I tasted every pill and every drop of whiskey, and I know your pain."

Ryan gazed into the King's eyes for eternity and a day and knew it to be true.

Finally, the King broke the silence.

"One day, it will come untrue. As it did for the Dying Lands. So it will for you. In fact, from my perspective, it already has. Everything has been made new."

Then, quick and simple as that, He walked back over to His desk, picked up the book He was writing, and headed for the bookshelves. Ryan turned. Walls and walls of books. Endless. Forever. Stories without measure, worlds without end, all contained within the pages of the books of the King.

"What story is that?"

"Yours," the King replied. "Well, part of it, anyway."

He put it on a half-full shelf.

"The rest of your story I am still writing. It's a real corker."

The King suddenly seemed to be the only thing that existed. The only thing that had ever existed. The books melted away. The stars fell from the sky. Suns turned to blood, kingdoms crumbled, grass grew, rains fell, darkness conquered all. Only the King remained. Then the train of His robe filled the room, and voices cried out in holy fear, and smoke consumed all, and the idea that the Creator of All Things was ever a vision of a small, frail, human king seemed a laughable blasphemy.

Ryan's curiosity got the better of him. With great effort, he looked in the direction of the furious brightness where the King had once stood.

Ryan instantly dropped dead. But he did not hit the ground. He kept falling.

CHAPTER 20:

HOME

There are two ways of getting home; and one of them is to stay there. The other is to walk round the whole world till we come back to the same place.

—G. K. Chesterton, *The Everlasting Man*

Have you ever watched one of those YouTube videos where people with way too much time on their hands launch potatoes through glass windows or shoot bullets through bananas in slow motion? They're quite fascinating. I once spent an entire year—in your human reckoning, of course—just watching bizarre YouTube videos.[60] There's something mesmerizing about watching a piece of fruit get absolutely obliterated by a small piece of metal shot out of a pressurized cylinder using a small, controlled explosion.

Anyway, that's what Ryan's body looked like as it rocketed out of the Dying Lands, up, up, up through space and time, cracking the edge of reality and bursting through the end of the known universe and

---

[60] And by the way, if you don't believe that mankind is totally depraved, helplessly covered in sin from the moment of conception, all you have to do is go check out some YouTube comment sections for a few minutes. Seriously, what's wrong with you people?!

finding himself in another one altogether. And then another. And then another. Your own reality is actually only thirty-seven realities away from the Dying Lands. So you're practically next-door neighbors. Traveling to Universe 781-C-2, for instance, can take a human consciousness over five billion years, which is longer than you think it is. So Ryan got pretty lucky, in that traveling just thirty-seven realities only takes about 0.0000007 seconds in your world, though it feels like a good sixty seconds to the person who is being very uncomfortably shot through multiple realities like—well, like a bullet through thirty-seven bananas.

Ryan suddenly woke up on a purple church carpet with a pulverized projector by his head, surrounded by hysterical parishioners.

The next few months were a blur. As you might have expected, Ryan never went back to Ignite Christian Collective, though they did send him a note of apology and a check for $570 so he would not sue them.

He did, however, return to church, several more times. He found a smaller one that used hymnals instead of projectors. He'd made several calls ahead of time to confirm with the pastor that there were no projectors, especially not ones hanging from the ceiling. One bright Sunday morning, he drove his beat-up Honda Civic into the much smaller parking lot of a much smaller church.

"Hi," said a voice as Ryan took his first few steps toward the small building of faded stucco and chipped blue paint. He turned.

A woman with red hair and bright green eyes stood there. She looked familiar, but Ryan couldn't place her.

"Hi," he said. "I don't want any visitor swag or anything. I've been here before."

"I don't work here or anything," she said. "I was just saying hi. I'm new around here."

"Oh, OK. Well, I'm heading in."

"Alright. See you in there," she replied.

He stood awkwardly, staring at her a little too long, wondering where he'd seen her before.

"Are you OK?" she asked.

"Yeah. Yeah, I think so."

The red-haired girl stuck out her hand. "My name's Faith."

Ryan looked her up and down, feeling as though he knew her from somewhere. He froze, suddenly realizing he had been staring at her way too long.

"What?" she asked. "Seriously, are you OK?"

"Yeah, sorry. I'm new here too."

"Well, don't make it weird or anything," she said, smiling. "I can go in with you if you want."

"Sure, I guess that'd be nice."

She laughed, and for a moment—just a moment—Ryan remembered.

A Final Word from the Narrator

I'm a chronicler of stories, as you well know by now. I'm writing the last few words of this book at this very moment. Thanks for sticking with me all the way to the end! Soon, the ink will dry on this final page, and I can close it up and put it on the shelf.

What a story this one was! Sometimes I get assigned to really boring stuff like watching *The View* and writing that down. *Yuck*. Nobody up here likes *View* duty. So I was glad the Creator trusted me enough to chronicle the epic tale of Ryan Fleming, thirty-three, of the San Fernando Valley, and his 3.28-second-long dream on the floor of Ignite Christian Collective.

I told you earlier that I had no idea why God chose Ryan for this particular quest. Ryan's not the one I would have chosen. There are 2.7 billion humans currently alive who are more qualified for this journey. I didn't expect much from such an unimpressive guy. I sometimes find myself sneering at the people our Creator chooses to pour out His grace upon. But in thousands of years of chronicling stories of different beings in different universes, He's never failed to surprise me. Sometimes the stories are cut short by unexpected tragedy. Most of the time, the heroes fail, throwing the gifts and grace of their Creator spitefully in the dirt. Yet He never stops reaching out. He never stops pouring out grace. I find myself filled with awe and wonder at the stories He allows His creatures to create alongside Him. I long to look into these mysteries more, but an eternity would never be enough.

What happened to Ryan changed him forever. It wasn't an instant shift in his life, and he wasn't immediately a different person. It was a slow change, effected by small moments and baby steps and the Author of All Stories piercing time and space and pulling Ryan, inch by inch, toward Himself so he could take part in the greatest story ever told.

Who was that girl on the last page? Was that Faith? Did she show up in your world? How did that happen? Sadly, I'm not at liberty to say. It's what we call an "ambiguous ending," such as the top spinning in *Inception* or the ending of *Blade Runner* not really telling you if Deckard was a replicant.[61] Did Ryan "get saved" and become a Christian and live happily ever after? Once again, not part of this story and well above my pay grade. If you want answers to these questions, write a letter to the publisher demanding a sequel. Maybe that will help.

I'm a chronicler of stories. And maybe the next one will be yours. The next time you have a crazy dream, whether you're falling off a cliff into a pile of kittens, wielding a sword in an epic battle against aliens with deadly laser-pincers for the fate of some far-off distant world, or you're shrunk to the size of a thimble and discover your yard is a world of adventures all by itself, maybe it's a true story. And maybe I'll be your Narrator.

Or maybe it was just a bad burrito.

---

[61] Since I finished Ryan's story, I've become pretty obsessed with human cinema. I've watched thousands of your films now. I've put a request in with the higher-ups to get an answer to these two films, but no answer as of yet.

ACKNOWLEDGEMENTS

The authors would together like to thank the extraordinarily talented Laurel Sprenger for her gorgeous illustrations, the awesome Jamie Foley for her hard work on the map, and the meticulous (and only slightly desperate) Kristin Oren for her feedback and edits. And thank you to Seth Dillon and the rest of the incredible team at The Babylon Bee, all the fine folks at Salem Books, and our agent, Steve Laube, for helping us make this crazy idea a reality.

Joel would like to thank his beautiful wife Kelsey—who stuck with him through doubts and failures and encouraged him to start writing; his kids, who begged him each night to read one more chapter; Kyle Mann, for his daily encouragement, partnership, and friendship; The Babylon Bee for changing his life; and his Creator, who pours out grace upon grace every single day.

Kyle would like to thank his wife Destiny; his three boys, Emmett, Samuel, and Calvin; and the rest of his great big family: Mom, Dad,

Ryan, Karis, Megan, and all their wonderful kids and spouses, and his early readers/guinea pigs Suzanne Sowada and Justin Rasmusson. And a big thanks to God for creating coffee, without which this book would never have seen the light of day.

Also by Kyle, Joel, & The Babylon Bee

How to Be a Perfect Christian
The Sacred Texts of The Babylon Bee
The Babylon Bee Guide to Wokeness
The Babylon Bee Guide to Democracy